A DREAM OF TREASON

By Marshall Pugh

COMMANDER CRABB

A WILDERNESS OF MONKEYS

THE CHANCER

STRANGER ANY PLACE

THE LAST PLACE LEFT

A MURMUR OF MUTINY

A DREAM OF TREASON

A DREAM OF TREASON

by

MARSHALL PUGH

COWARD, McCANN & GEOGHEGAN, INC.
New York

for Strang

A DREAM OF TREASON

1

On his way uptown by car from Wall Street on his last day
in New York, John Middlemass saw the church notice board
with the instant sermon *If you're feeling happy, let your face
know.* A Jewish joke on a Christian chapel. The poster
looked as if it had been on show for years but he had not
noticed it before. The situation he had created was heighten-
ing his perception, it was a little like falling in love.

Earlier that day he had looked up into a high sky, an almost Spanish sky in the annual miracle of fall and he had
remembered that he was leaving the first city he had ever
liked. And so he was more than normally aware of life on the
sidewalk beyond the car and he wondered if he had been
wrong about the women of the city. Maybe they didn't have
the strangest legs this side of Paris. A Hari Krishna gaggle
went honking by, apparently unaware that their religion was
doomed and that their god had gone away. Two blacks sepa-
rated solemnly to make way for them, then giggled when they
had passed, dissolving into happy African laughter in the
streets of New York. . . .

As he looked in the driver's mirror, Middlemass saw the
car behind them pull into the side. A parked car made way
for a third. It was more than thirty years since Middlemass

had been hunted and the antics of the shadowing cars amused him. The rules had changed but the game was the same. As a fourth car began tracking him on the road home, which he had taken most evenings for years, he restrained the desire to laugh. Middlemass was aware of his fierce and sombre face; he could never look lighthearted and he didn't want to worry his driver.

"You think we're being tailed, Ray?"

"I don't think it, I know it." The driver looked calm, almost bored; he had been as carefully selected as the rest of Middlemass' small staff. To a man they reflected his dislike of servility and his hatred of ostentation or the trappings of power. The driver was unobtrusively powerful, like the car. "I'll lose them soon," he said.

"Don't," Middlemass said. "Drop me here and go home."

"Me?"

"You." An order was not a basis for discussion. "I'll see you."

"I hope so, Mr. Middlemass. Is that all?"

"That's all." He got out and idled on the sidewalk to watch the tailing car as it hugged the side, dropping speed steadily until the metal sheep behind it started bleating. Then he ambled slowly homeward.

Just short of his apartment on Central Park West, he changed direction and made for the crumbling dark tenements behind. As he crossed one of the more abrupt frontiers in New York, he wasn't afraid of being mugged. In the past he hadn't exactly gone out of his way to avoid such an encounter. So far no thief had expected a man of Middlemass' age or appearance to be so useful with his feet. None had ever come fast enough or thought of protecting his balls. In this street Middlemass was usually left alone and he was pleasantly surprised when the old woman stopped him. Her ragged coat was pinned where the buttons should have been. "Anything you want for five dollars," she said.

"I don't want anything," Middlemass said. He had been aware of his Linguaphone accent ever since he heard his recorded voice on the radio. He spoke nine languages too well—he suspected that he sounded bogus even when he spoke in his native tongue. "Nothing much," he said and the old woman laughed in his face. "I'll give you the five if you'll stand here and talk with me a little." The old woman's laughter choked and she stared into his face, trying to work out what kind of pervert he was.

"Talk?" she asked.

"That's all." But she didn't seem much of a conversationalist and he wondered if he should try to keep it interesting by lecturing her on the wicked life she led. "You often do this?" he asked. "You often accost middle-aged men?"

"Yeah, do you?" she asked. "Or young guys?"

"Not too often. I prefer mature company, myself." The tail had a problem; he was wrongly dressed for a slow stroll on that street. As the shadow stopped in a doorway, a hidden drunk jeered at him and he crossed to the far side. Middlemass figured this was a junior operator and he felt a certain sympathy, for he had once shadowed dangerous men without a cover and without enough experience, himself. . . .

"This what you call talking?" the old woman asked.

"I want to ask you something but it isn't too easy," Middlemass said. "You look sensitive to me."

"Sensitive? What do you mean, sensitive?" she asked. "That some kind of crack?" The man who was following Middlemass walked by uncertainly on the far side of the street. "Screw you, you pervert."

"Anything you say." He gave the old woman five dollars then began to follow his shadow. He knew he wasn't playing

11

fair, and that this man had probably been bundled out of a tailing car without a proper briefing. In spite of that, Middlemass was not ashamed of his pleasure in the unexpected call to bush league.

As he walked behind the tail, he reminded himself that he was out of practise, and that he had to start somewhere to get the feel of the park again. Since no normal adult would earn his living in counterespionage in peacetime, the opposition recruited children of all ages. So he had to retrain himself in their way of thinking. He wanted to win this game and if he tried playing as an adult, he might lose. But he lacked his old protection of healthy fear for he believed he had nothing to lose beyond the game. . . .

As his pursuer faltered at the corner, Middlemass stopped behind him and lit a cigarette. Indecisively, the man turned the corner, reached the wine store and studied the bottles in the window. When Middlemass stopped behind him, the man went into the store with Middlemass at his back.

The wine store had everything for the people who already had everything, the people on Central Park West. Middlemass had never understood why the neighbouring poor did not set that store on fire or at least break a window now and then. The agent seemed in no hurry with his shopping so Middlemass bought a bottle of vodka so deeply frozen that it didn't look as if it could be cracked open until the icebreakers came with the spring. On cue the other man picked up a bottle of wine and handed over the money. Middlemass tapped his shadow on the shoulder and the man almost dropped his wine. He was young, muscular and much taller than Middlemass but his military moustache was downy, not much of a success.

"Excuse me," Middlemass said, "Wine interests me. Can I see the label?"

The agent automatically handed him the bottle marked Beaujolais.

"Beaujolais. Well, it's a wine-producing region. But this isn't a Moulin-a-Vent. I don't believe that this bottle justifies its price." While he talked, Middlemass was looking for distinctive features of a forgettable face that would not register character for years to come. The feeble moustache would not survive and the most remarkable thing about him was his hair, so closely cropped that Middlemass wondered if he could play tennis on that head. He wanted the agent to answer, so that he could record the voice but the man silently replaced the savaged Beaujolais and bought a bottle of sparkling Portuguese rosé.

"Haven't we met before?" Middlemass asked him.

"No, sir, I don't think so." The agent had an unexpectedly deep voice.

"You're certain?"

"I'm sure." As he began to walk away, Middlemass got between him and the door.

"My name is Middlemass," he said. "Maybe you haven't seen me before but I've seen you."

"I've really got to go."

"Yes. The young have always somewhere to go. Especially when they work for Matthew Sleet."

He got the reaction he wanted, for Matthew Sleet was a senior man in the opposition.

"I don't know anybody named Sleet," the agent said. "Let me by, will you?" Middlemass let him go, for he had served his purpose, and the news would soon reach Matthew Sleet that Middlemass knew he was being watched. As he walked back to his apartment, he calculated that the hounds would be called off for the moment and he needed a respite. Within an hour he would be talking to his daughter, Shona. Although the war of the generations had been on for them for years, there were signs Shona might be willing to sign a separate peace. Arrangements had to be made and things to be said, things she might remember later. . . .

The new elevator man wore the normal grey suit and cap, but his uniform was ill-fitting, and he pressed the right button without asking which floor Middlemass wanted. As usual that silent elevator made Middlemass think of a crematorium coffin travelling the wrong way. "Charlie out sick again?" he asked.

"Charlie, sir?" The operator had an expensive accent.

"Charlie. The usual man. The Pole."

"He's not too well again, sir."

"The old trouble?" Middlemass asked, raising the vodka bottle.

"You've got it, sir," the operator said. "He just can't leave it alone." Middlemass sighed and the elevator man shook his head in sorrow, although the usual man was named Manolo and he was an unusual Puerto Rican, a lifetime teetotaller.

Middlemass felt cheated as the elevator gate closed behind him. The standard of play among the opposition was not high and he wondered if Matthew Sleet was closely involved, after all.

His apartment door had three locks, which he'd secured when he left that morning, but one was open now and Middlemass held the door for a moment. As always the lights were on, for his housekeeper believed the Con Ed commercial that wasting electricity kept thieves away. As Middlemass sniffed he caught the sweet niff of Virginian tobacco, although he smoked Gauloise, his housekeeper did not smoke at all and Middlemass had no more staff in the bare, unloved apartment, which reflected his lack of interest in personal possessions.

He threw the main switch, blacking out the apartment. Then he took the vodka bottle by the neck, as he decided that the bathroom off the hall was the most strategic hiding place. The man could wait there until the owner moved into the kitchen or the main rooms beyond. So Middlemass slammed the front door, walked through and slammed the kitchen door, then moved back quietly to wait. As time passed and his visitor made no move, Middlemass wondered whether his imagination was working overtime. By now any professional thief would have decided that this apartment wasn't worth his trouble. Perhaps the intruder was less of a fool, more skilful than the other agents. . . .

The bathroom door opened slowly, the man poked his head into the hall and Middlemass gave him the vodka full strength on the back of his head. He was surprised when the bottle splintered, he surmised that the icing process had made it fragile but he had never been strong on physics. The man fell so fast that Middlemass missed when he shoved a foot out to break the drop. As he switched on the lights, he heard the elevator returning.

The elevator man tried the door and he ignored him. The fallen agent was in a bad way. Pieces of broken glass were sticking from his head and the blood was ruining the carpet. Middlemass wasn't worried about that carpet personally but he knew that his housekeeper would care. He was annoyed with himself, he had intended only to question the man, then drop a hint for the ear of Matthew Sleet. He bolted the front door just before the elevator man tried to force it.

"Get the police," Middlemass shouted.

"Sir?"

"The police. I've caught a thief."

"A thief, sir? Let me help you."

15

"The police. I'd call a squad car but they never seem to make it inside the hour."

"Let me in . . . sir."

"Run down the block and get the cop on the beat."

"Can I phone from your apartment, sir?"

"Move. You'll need an ambulance, too."

Middlemass was pleased to hear him running. There would now be a short delay while the elevator man contacted base for new orders. When he examined the agent closely, he was relieved to find he was breathing, for a corpse in the apartment wouldn't be too convenient. Although he knew his telephone was tapped, he phoned the police and gave the desk sergeant a quick rundown on the affair, acting out the melodrama for whoever was listening. The sergeant was still asking questions when Middlemass left his phone off the hook and walked away. He didn't have the time or the inclination to remove the glass and bathe the skull. Instead he frisked the man, pocketed his heavy .358 magnum and his ID card. It was pathetic that they should carry such paper crutches. The man had probably flashed it at his mother-in-law or even his wife when his movements were being questioned. Then Middlemass got up and kicked the broken glass away as he thought out his next move.

Four cars had trailed him and he'd made direct contact with three agents. Obviously this was prime time for the Middlemass hunt and he had to move. So he wrote a note for the police, apologising for his absence. He said that he was suffering from shock, that he had gone to the drugstore to buy more tranquilisers. It was too poor a story even to convince a policeman but he didn't have the patience to concoct a better lie. Then he left the note for the police on the agent's chest and put his personal letter to Matthew Sleet in the man's pocket. Middlemass had always wanted that note to go by hand, but he hadn't expected such a fast delivery.

Cautiously he unbolted the door, checked for sounds or smells, then headed for the elevator, which was open and empty. The chances were that the operator had deliberately stalled it while he was talking to his base. Once more Middlemass was distressed by their lack of training. Surely Sleet was getting slack? He closed the doors, dropped to the basement and ran through the heating complex to the rear door, which led up and out into an alley.

Fortunately Otsch Gellner, his doctor and his friend, did not live far away. Middlemass calculated he would be safer to go on foot. It wasn't worth the risk of walking into a well-lit street to hail a cab.

2

DOCTOR GELLNER'S FOURTH WIFE showed him into their apartment and, hard as he tried, Middlemass could not remember her given name. He had never acquired the American gift of remembering names easily, for his highly selective memory bank rejected such information.

"I'm sorry, Mrs. Gellner," Middlemass said, "Otsch is expecting me and . . ."

". . . and he'll be back any minute." She nodded to the question he hadn't asked, showed him into the living room, then vanished. Mrs. Gellner looked worried and gaunt, with too many miles on her clock. Despite his age, Gellner was still wearing out wives and trading them in for newer models.

Otsch Gellner would have to leave his apartment as part of the settlement, a serious impediment to the divorce, for the doctor had taken time to find a place close to his office and quiet, in a canyon created by four tall buildings.

Besides, Gellner could never again re-create this living room. The walls were sombre, the furniture was heavy, the only painting was of fir trees and the samovar in the corner was bright with nostalgia. This was an exact replica of the room in East Prussia, which Gellner had left forever, one night in 1934. . . .

"Well, now," Gellner said, "I was wondering when you'd show up." His velvet smoking jacket and his gold-rimmed glasses were in keeping with the room. "I've had a visit from one of your colleagues, another financier."

"Another what?"

"Don't worry," Gellner said. "I know you don't have colleagues. You'd play baseball on your own if you could."

"So who was he?"

"A large fat man with a still face and very active eyes. Matthew Sleet?"

"What did he want?"

"Relax," Gellner said, "he didn't get it. He told me your close friends were worried about your mental state."

"And you agreed, Otsch?"

"I could have said your closest friends have worried about your mental state for thirty years. But you're sane enough," Gellner said, "it's a bigger question." Gellner still could not pronounce the word "question" correctly and Middlemass wondered why they always talked in English with Gellner sounding like Herr Doktor Disney and Middlemass like an earnest language student. But it was too old a habit to change.

"I didn't help him very much."

"Thanks, Otsch. You've got my papers?"

"Would I sell them?"

"Thanks. I haven't got much time." He told Gellner about the intruder.

"He was searching for the papers, I suppose?"

"The place was clean weeks ago. Wish I hadn't hit him so hard."

Gellner cleaned his spectacles. "You never miss the chance to hit somebody hard. But they'll be looking for you harder."

20

"Maybe. . . . If Sleet calls again, I came to see you. All right?"

"Yes."

"I was in a nervous state and you decided to hospitalise **me** overnight," Middlemass said.

"Hospitalise? Must you use that odious expression?"

"You sent me off in a taxi. It wasn't your fault that I never showed up at the hospital. Too much to ask?"

"No, but I have a trifling condition. I want to know why you are being followed by the CIA."

"Too dangerous. For you."

"Let me decide. The Gestapo couldn't break me."

"You were younger then, Otsch."

"And so were you. It's about this oil concession you haven't got?"

"I'll get it, Otsch."

"The Sultan of Doha could change his mind. Arabs often do."

"He won't, Otsch. And I'm not giving the Doha oil to the States. I'm selling to the Japanese."

Gellner looked impressed and he wasn't easily impressed. "All that oil? Enough to support the unbearable life we lead? Why take such a risk?"

"I'm putting loyalty to my investors first. My dividends right or wrong."

Gellner found that funny. "Loyalty to your investors," he said. "So suddenly? Shall I explain to you?"

"Save it. Some other time."

"You don't want to die in bed. You're doing this for fun. . . . What do they call it? Black comedy? Or Black farce?"

"Maybe, Otsch. I'll have to go."

"You want to die violently," Gellner said. "Better an end in horror than a horror without end."

21

Middlemass was shocked, he had not expected Gellner to quote Hitler.

"You've made your mark on the world but you want to make it deeper, make it last. And that's something I've always known."

Gellner produced the papers from his jacket. "I took the liberty of glancing at them," he said. "The passport's an excellent forgery."

"Thanks. I'd have one done for you but I haven't got the time."

Doctor Gellner handed over his car keys. "Take my car and leave the keys in the trunk. It's self-locking."

"No thanks."

"Take it." Gellner spoke sharply. "I'll tell them you went to the hospital in my car. They'll find it at some airport, I suppose."

"Not an airport." He gave Gellner an address near the Lower East Side.

"That's fine," Gellner said. "If the police can't find it, I'll stumble on it myself." He showed his friend to the door. "Your other motive," Gellner said. "You've got a natural gift for intrigue and treachery. . . ."

"Kind of you."

"It's not as unkind as you think. You've suppressed it too long. It's dangerous to smother such an impulse."

"Good, I'll indulge it then." Middlemass clapped Gellner's shoulder and held the front door. "There's one other *little* thing." He handed Gellner an envelope sealed with the wax impression of his ring, the ring he found so useful in self-defence. "If I don't survive the next month, will you deliver this, personally?"

Gellner read the address with distaste. "I don't want to meet him. He's the noisiest whistle-blower in the country."

"But you'll do it?"

"I may wear dark glasses so I don't have to see him too clearly. But suppose something happens to me?"

"You're the end of the line," Middlemass said. "Four more letters go off automatically if I'm not around to stop them. All addressed to loud whistlers. If Sleet's crazy enough to arrest you, tell him that. Don't be brave. You won't know anything he doesn't."

Gellner turned the letter over and held it up to the light, parodying a check for a counterfeit bill. "What's in it?"

"Come on. You can open it without damaging the seal. And you'll do that." Gellner was still studying the envelope as he leaned against the door.

"Naturally," he said, "but I want to know now."

"It's about the Presidency. That subject always bores you."

"Not now. The President still has secrets?"

Middlemass practised breathing control, remembering that Gellner had won most of their arguments in wartime Europe and the resistance.

"Some," he said. "This is a list of some of the people he's had killed and how and why he did it."

Gellner sighed, opened the door and waved his old friend through. "Your own name is on the list?"

"Not yet. Not before I close the Doha deal and that's all the time I need."

"Sleet was right," Gellner said. "You're mad."

They walked in silence to the garage then Gellner opened his car door and handed over the keys. "This is a dead man's gesture, nothing more," he said. "And it's so futile. You're not going to die . . . if you stop this nonsense now. You don't have to behave like the generals in the bunker. That was why I quoted Hitler but you didn't get the point."

"Didn't I?"

"You're not dying of cancer. The tumour was benign. How much more proof do you need?"

"I know the tumour was benign."

"You know it but you don't believe it. You haven't changed a lot in thirty years. How am I going to convince you?" Gellner was talking faster. "I've been telling you the truth. I wouldn't lie to you about the tumour."

"I know that." Middlemass started the engine but Gellner stood in the way.

"You may know with your brain perhaps. But not with your instincts. How often have I told you that the word 'instinct' is meaningless?"

"Too often." Middlemass had learned to trust his intuitions.

"Not often enough. Your instinct says you won't live long. Every year you expect to be your last."

"That's true of most intelligent adults nowadays," Middlemass said. "You mind if I go?"

"In a moment. You and I didn't have much chance of surviving the war. If we'd followed your instincts . . ."

"Otsch. Will you get out of the way? Suppose we talk about the war another time."

"There won't be another time," Gellner said. "You remember me asking you what you'd do if you knew you were going to die? This was in Prague."

"I don't remember," Middlemass said, for he had cultivated the art of forgetting and pulled down the blind on the war and the Gestapo. Despite him, that blind would run up from time to time and he would break out in a sweat on a cold day.

Marshall Pugh

"We talked about what to do if we were certain of death, even of a kindly death in bed. And you said?"

"I don't recall."

"You said you'd cheat death. You'd commit suicide right away."

3

MIDDLEMASS STOPPED THE CAR and looked up at the power station on the East River. He hadn't been so close to it in years and even now it didn't look real to him; he still saw it as a location shot in a New York movie. When he had parked Gellner's car, he locked the keys in the trunk and walked toward the river.

East Fourteenth Street was not familiar territory but he recognised the brick stockade on the north side of the street with its guards and its metal gates, which were closed against reality. Ray, his driver, had once lived there and hated it, called it a middle-class ghetto.

On the south were the brownstone walk-ups where his daughter Shona lived with her troubled friends and their problems. She had majored in sociology, she took her work seriously, but her charity began when she left home. Shona had written him off as a selfish loner, a bad father and a worse husband before her mother died. Afterward the gap had widened and he'd never been able to cross the chasm to East Fourteenth. Now she had written him while he was planning this final deal and he had made a formal appointment.

The house number showed above an elaborate display of trash cans but he didn't know the floor where Shona lived.

27

There was a light under the badly fitting door on the ground floor and a young Puerto Rican answered his knock. He had a gentle, puzzled face; he seemed to be wondering what he was doing in New York.

"Shona Middlemass?" the Puerto Rican said. "She live here all right but she's not in as of now. She told me to watch out for her father. You her father? Good to meet you, Mister. Step inside." He was named Narcisso, his mother was Pacquita and Middlemass lost track of the names of the younger children in this one-room apartment divided into male and female sleeping quarters.

The place wasn't just clean, it was burnished and Narcisso waved him into a chair heady with the smell of polish. It was quiet in the room, the mother was cooking while the younger children divided their attention between Middlemass and the television, which had been turned down in honour of the guest. "You're a friend of Shona's?"

"Everybody here's a friend of Shona," Narcisso said. "You're welcome."

"Thanks. Did she say when she'd be back?"

"No, sir. She just asked me to look out for you and give you the key to her apartment. You understand how to work a police lock? No? I'll show you. She wants you to make yourself right at home."

They passed the padlocked john on the second floor, then Narcisso showed Middlemass how to operate the lock. "And this is the key to the toilet," he said. "If you're going in there, lock up behind you but leave the phone off the hook. If somebody calls you, he'll call back."

For a moment habit almost betrayed Middlemass into offering money but he stopped his hand in time and showed Narcisso out with Spanish courtesy. Then he fiddled with the police lock, which reminded him of pulp crime magazines.

Middlemass had little capacity for introspection or self-pity, but while he wandered around the apartment, he wondered why the split with Shona had been so savage. The main door opened on the kitchen, which had a bath in the corner in obedience to the laws; the bath made the cold-water apartment into a hot-water establishment. The kitchen heater was primitive but effective, an old hairdryer that blew warm air in winter, cool in summer. Beyond the bath, its shower curtain and its rotted pipe, there were shelves with an impressive display of pots and cooking utensils. Middlemass had almost forgotten she was interested in cooking for other people, as her mother had been. Neither of them had eaten much themselves. As he scanned the kitchen, he remembered without guilt what a bitch her mother had been. He believed it was worse to think ill of the living than of the dead. One day Shona might know more about her mother. . . .

He blocked that line of thought before it had properly formed and diverted his attention to the noisy icebox, stacked with food. Its top held enough bottles to stock the average bar. Shona didn't drink much but she liked to be hospitable and he wondered where she found the money for the liquor when she was entertaining her friends and listening to their troubles.

The police lock rattled and he opened up, expecting Shona. But the girl in the doorway was smaller and older with a sheepdog hairstyle that didn't quite hide the lines that had arrived too early. "You've just got to be Shona's father," she said. "I knew you right away. Shona said you looked like a soldier of fortune. I'm Rachel. Good to know you." Rachel shook hands briskly, walked by him and ransacked the icebox, loading cartons into a plastic laundry bag. "This stuff is mine, I swear it," she said. "I live right below and Shona lets me use her icebox. You believe me, don't you?"

"Why not?" He wondered why they were so obsessed with security locks. Clearly they trusted each other much more than his neighbours on Central Park did. "You think she'll be long?"

"She'll be here," Rachel said. "You know you look like an actor? But I can't remember which one." She explained how the police lock functioned in greater detail than Narcisso, said, "Ciao," then left Middlemass to prowl through the apartment.

The bedroom had a double bed and, from the electric razor on the shelf, it looked as if it had been used as a double. He had expected to mind about that, but he didn't. He only wanted to meet the man and talk to him over a drink.

. The living room was also interesting. In her Dadaist phase, Shona had fixed up a child's swing in a corner and some fool had swung it in and cracked the ceiling. The paintings on the walls were new to him but he recognized her work, particularly a strange asexual creature dressed in white in a jungle of flowers. As he looked closer, he saw that she had written *for one night or the other night will come the gardener in white and gathered flowers are dead, Yasmin.* As he looked more closely at the gardener in white, Middlemass remembered how he had slept with his head beneath the sheets when he was small. He liked his daughter's work, he believed she might make a living as a painter. But did she always have to let this eerie quality intrude?

The door rattled, the police lock held. "You there, Dad?" Shona called. The form of address was a relief. When she was angry with him, she called him "Daddy" and made it sound like "my lord."

Shona was twenty now and more beautiful than he'd remembered. She was tall but so cunningly constructed that you didn't notice her height until you stood beside her.

"Casing the joint?" she asked. "Turning over my drum?" She was smiling but it was not a warm smile as she showed the strong white teeth that were still slightly slanted. Middlemass was glad he'd insisted on braces when she was small.

"No, I wasn't searching your place," Middlemass said. "And where did you pick up the English slang?"

"The usual way, from a sleeping dictionary," she said.

"An *Englishman?*" he asked.

"Sorry if that bothers you. I didn't know the colour bar applied."

"I'd like to meet him, that's all . . ."

"Sorry, I can't arrange that," she said. "He isn't around anymore. Anyway he was a professional Englishman. New York's lousy with them, you know that." He also knew by her vehemence that she missed this man. "You don't like phonies, do you, Dad? Sincerity's your bag."

Middlemass sat down and studied the cracked ceiling. Less than five minutes in the room and she was trying to provoke him, but he refused to oblige. This was the last time he'd see her at home. Even if he pulled off the deal and lived . . . for a while . . . he could never come back to the States.

"I'm sorry," Shona said as she watched him.

"For what?"

"I said I was sorry. What more do you want?"

"A drink," her father said.

"Vodka?"

"Anything but vodka." His memory punched up the picture of the bleeding head and the broken vodka bottle.

"Whiskey?" she asked. She produced a single malt, a Glenlivet, and she saw him reading the label.

"I haven't gone wild," she said. "He left it. He bought it at London Airport coming out, cost him two eighty. He owes me a lot more than that." Middlemass was so pleased she was

31

learning to price things. For the first eighteen years of her life, Shona knew the value of nothing. She had always been generous, which was easy, for money wasn't real to her. It came from a bottomless spring.

"So I'm living better than I was," she said. "Most of your money goes out but I keep enough to live on."

"You're cashing my cheques? When did you start?" He was pleased but puzzled.

"Months ago. Don't you ever check your bank account? No, you don't have to, do you? I got around to it in the end. I can use your money in this job. So why not?"

"Why not?" Middlemass raised his glass. "Is that why you wrote?"

"Yes and no," she said. He noticed that she handled the Glenlivet bottle like a dead rat and poured herself a glass of table wine. "I had to see Otsch Gellner. It was an abortion, a very young girl, and I wanted his advice. He gave me the general impression you were in some kind of trouble." She spoke casually but her eyes betrayed her. "Are you in trouble, Dad?"

"Some. Nothing much. I don't want to talk about it now."

"What's more important?" Shona asked. She sat down and showed the worn knees in her jeans. Middlemass knew she had to dress for the job, but . . .

"I'm asking you, what's more important, Dad?"

"I don't think you'd be any happier if you knew," he said.

"I've got to go away for a while and I wanted to see you, that's all."

"Arabia again?"

"England," he said. "Like your friend."

"You kidding? He'll never leave America until they throw him out. Why England?"

"Business," he said. "I want to talk about you."

Shona finished her glass of wine, made a face, forgot her revulsion at the Glenlivet and poured herself a glass. "And I want to talk about us," she said. "I'm getting old, you know?"

"You're getting what?"

"I'm pushing twenty-one, Dad."

"Practically your prime."

"Listen to me, don't try to put me down. It wasn't just the cheques and it wasn't only what Otsch Gellner said . . . or didn't say. There's something else. I owe you an apology."

"You don't. All right, you do. I accept it."

"Will you *please* listen? I still get edgy when you're around and I'm still rude to you, but that's out of habit, that's all and I'm sorry."

"Don't be," he said. "And don't try to kick the habit now."

"You aren't telling me anything, are you, Dad? But you want to. Stop hinting. Talk. And there's something *you* have to know. Remember the fight we had over Mother's things?"

"No," he said abruptly.

"Yes you do. You were going to burn her papers and I grabbed them."

"I don't remember."

"You do. Anyway, I kept the letters. Then one night, I don't know what got into me, I read them."

"You said you wouldn't do that."

"I didn't mean to," she said, "but I thought they'd be all sweetness and light."

He got up and turned his back, pretending to look for the water jug. "So I read them. All the men, all the cheap tricks, all the bogus romance. Why didn't you tell me she was like that?"

"Don't ask stupid questions, Shona."

"You could have defended yourself."

"Only by nailing her up. You expect me to do that? At your age?"

"You always were a bastard," she said. "But it was out and in the open. But she . . . ah . . . the hell with it."

"The hell with it," he said. "Listen, I've made some arrangements and . . ."

"Me, too. I've arranged to find out what you're doing, Dad. Will you stop looking at your watch? I'll let you know the time. Every five minutes I'll reset the buzzer."

"Fine," he said. "And go easy on that scotch you don't like." He told her almost as much as he'd told Gellner.

"Oh, Jesus," Shona said. "I don't have to ask you why. You've always had this self-destructive thing. But can't you stop it? Can't you turn back?"

"Not now," he said.

"Anyway, you hit a cop," she said, "with a vodka bottle. I knew I'd be proud of you *one* day." He was aware of the excitement, the hint of mischief in her face. She looked like her mother, she was trying to be a useful member of society, but she was still his daughter.

"I didn't hit a cop. A man from a different outfit."

"A more dangerous outfit," she said.

"They've been pretty amateurish so far."

As Shona rose, she didn't seem to notice that she'd spilled her drink. She sat in the child's swing and rocked it; then he knew who had cracked the ceiling. "Maybe I'd better come with you. They owe me a vacation."

"Sorry, but that's out." For years he'd been suggesting taking her anywhere at any time, so that they could be together to talk, a few thousand miles from the memory of her mother. "It's a dirty business. And a daughter with a conscience is the last thing I need."

"Maybe my conscience begins at home," she said. "But if you sell that oil to the Japanese instead of to the States . . . you'll be doing good, won't you?"

"Thanks," he said.

"I don't mean intentionally, Dad. I wouldn't insult you. But if the Japanese get a fair stake in Middle East oil, things might get cooler, no? A new power to help keep the peace out there? Less chance of a trade war if the Japanese get what they need."

"Don't count on a Nobel peace prize," he said.

"Does it matter why you're doing it, if it helps to cool the Middle East?"

"If," he said. " 'The last temptation is the greatest treason. To do the right deed for the wrong reason.' "

Shona got out of the swing as a flake of plaster dropped from the ceiling. "When did you get interested in Eliot?" she asked.

"Before you could read. I didn't think you'd recognise it. Isn't Eliot out of fashion?"

"So am I. I'm coming with you, Dad."

"You can't and that's final."

"You won't even tell me where you're going?"

"So long as you forget about it. A place called Rookwood. In Dorset."

"Rookwood?" she asked. "Laurence Adam?"

"You remember him? After ten years?"

"That creep. Talking about his house all the time. He made it sound like Versailles."

"It's a little smaller," he said. "But Versailles was never all that comfortable. That's why the Bourbons gave it up." He had chosen Rookwood House with care. The opposition might look for him in Arabia or with his Swiss backers in Zurich or even with his customers in Osaka. But no Bank of

England notes were involved, and even by *his* standards, his British staff was small. Rookwood house was near enough to London Airport and easily linked by radio with Zurich. But it was also on the Hampshire-Dorset border where the locals noticed the movements of every wandered sheep. Besides Laurence Adam would be honoured by his presence, and he was exceptionally stupid, as Shona had noticed when she was ten.

"I don't think Mr. Adam was wild about me, either," she said, "but we'll make out somehow."

"You won't," he said. "It so happens I'm going by charter flight and all the seats are taken."

"A charter flight? Why don't you row across? Make it really rugged."

He showed his forged passport and the ticket from the travel club for Australian dentists based in London. "They've had their walkabout in New York and they're heading back tonight. It seems London's lousy with Australian dentists practising on soft British teeth."

"So you won't be stopped at the airport?"

"Don't think so," he said. "They don't expect a hijacker with a charter load of dentists. Hope they don't ask about my upper left four."

"So I'll be your new assistant and I'll fly on the jump seat," she said.

"No," he said. "And I mean no. Can we drop it? So many other things we have to talk over."

"We can do that on the way," she said, suddenly resigned— too suddenly for his peace of mind. "I'll drive you to the airport. That's the least I can do. Wait here five minutes then come on down. And don't get caught in the lock."

Middlemass looked through the bookcases while he waited. Shona seemed to have a thing about Jane Austen, which surprised him, for he didn't think his daughter and the author had much in common. He checked his watch, wrote out a cheque, hid it under the wine bottle, fixed the police lock like an expert then walked downstairs. On the landing he met Rachel again. "I still can't think of the actor," she said. "But you sure do look like him."

Outside the house Shona was waiting in a battered Chevrolet. "What happened to the Lincoln?" he asked.

"Oh, come on, Dad. If I drove around this neighbourhood in a Lincoln, I'd get lynched."

"So you sent it back like the cheques?"

"Sorry but I sold it. The drug rehabilitation centre, it was very short of bread. But I kept enough for the Chevvy and a horn like the one in the Lincoln."

"Only the horn?"

"Yes, it was a terrific horn. I couldn't live without it. It was so melodious. D minor. Took me months to get a horn on the same note." She put on glasses to drive. Again this was new.

"You're going to be late getting home," he said.

"I'm always late home. But I'm driving carefully, okay? I'm not handling a car the way you do. It's just a Chevvy, right? It's not a train. And it burns too much gas when I go fast."

The ignoble thought occurred to him that his daughter was becoming as money-conscious as her mother had before her. She might want money for good causes but she still wanted money. Perhaps in trying to protect him, she was trying to protect the interests of her friends. . . .

"Stop thinking about money. Think about something serious," his daughter said, as the car reached the bridge.

"How did you know?"

"The way you were twisting your ring."

4

ON THE MORNING the execution was planned, Brigadier Richard Murray-Strachan awoke at six as usual, he hadn't needed an alarm clock in twenty years. Although he was to be executioner-in-chief, he had slept well and remembered nothing of his dreams. His masters had spoken, his protests had been overruled, the necessary act of taking out John Middlemass had been agreed. It only remained for Murray-Strachan to arrange the details and make some of his objections known to a wider audience. Normally he read for an hour before his working day began and he saw no reason to change his routine. But he could not concentrate on Runciman's history of the Crusades. When his telephone rang, he answered swiftly before his wife's sleep could be disturbed.

"Murray-Strachan," the brigadier said, for he could never bring himself to give his number, it made him feel like a recruit.

"Morning, *General*," the American said.

"And to you, Sleet," the brigadier replied.

"The target has reached England. Our arrangement stands, *General?*"

"It does, indeed," the brigadier said. "And by the way, Sleet . . ."

"Yes, General?"

"I do wish you wouldn't call me General. I'm only a humble brigadier."

"You surprise me," Sleet said. "I didn't think there was much humility in your nature." He hung up without waiting for the brigadier's reply. They were old acquaintances, they respected but distrusted each other and they had found that banter was safer than argument.

At the appointed hour the brigadier walked to the railway station with the tip of his umbrella beating out the time. Some senior soldiers in intelligence tried to look like civilians but Murray-Strachan suspected that they fooled no one but themselves. It was different for junior men but one couldn't wear a cloak and a funny nose in one's own village at one's age. So Murray-Strachan's city suit was immaculate, his bowler was brushed, his shoes caught the sun and his umbrella was furled like a flag.

At the station senior commuters nodded to him respectfully and he acknowledged by tipping up the point of his umbrella as he would have acknowledged a military salute. In the village it was generally believed that the brigadier had retired early and then taken some part-time job in military ordnance. Murray-Strachan had done nothing to dispel this rumour since he had started it himself. He felt hungry and then disturbed as he remembered that he had broken his routine. He had forgotten to whip up fresh eggs in milk, then drink the concoction, the one-minute breakfast he had enjoyed for so long.

As the train pulled in, he saw Lacey bearing down on him. Lacey was a fairly new man in the village, he sold motorcars at Shepherds Bush, or something of the kind. The man was inclined to talk on the train without encouragement or invitation. No doubt he would learn when he had put in some service on the line. And so the brigadier foreswore his usual corner seat, got in at the far end of the first-class compartment and cracked open his *Daily Telegraph.* Murray-Strachan rarely read the *Telegraph,* he preferred to study the left-wing press and find out what the other side was thinking, but he felt that the *Telegraph* fitted his image. Besides it was the right shape and size of newspaper to hide behind while he planned the day ahead.

For all that, the headline about the commercial potential of North Sea gas kept dancing and distracting him. Didn't those newspaper people know that all of the North Sea oil could not be gobbled up, that some of it had to be conserved as the reserve?

The train was well beyond Surbiton when Lacey had the audacity to move up the compartment and join him by sitting in a recently vacated seat.

"Good morning, sir," Lacey said.

"Good morning to *you,*" the brigadier replied, making Lacey a present of the day.

"Do you mind if I join you?"

"Good heavens, no," Murray-Strachan said. "But we'll be at Waterloo very shortly, I should think. Train's been on time all the way. Miracles sometimes happen, eh?"

"We've time enough," Lacey said and the brigadier stared at him along the sight of his newspaper. This man who refused to be put off by a polite refusal had unfortunate features in Murray-Strachan's view. Although he was in his mid-fifties, Lacey's mouth was still weak and wet, he had the air of a man who had passed from adolescence to early decay without an intervening phase of manhood. "My wife's hoping to ginger up the local Conservative Association," Lacey said.

"Is she, indeed?"

"And she rather wondered whether you would address them one night."

"Not much of a hand at speeches, myself," Murray-Strachan said. "Or at politics, come to that. What's the subject, may I ask?"

"She rather thought . . . the decline in authority, you know? More power for the police. The return of capital punishment and so on."

"How original, very." Murray-Strachan said. The train was passing the new fruit and vegetable market at Nine Elms; they were almost at Waterloo Station so the brigadier folded his newspaper with care and took his time to find space for it in his briefcase. "But I'm afraid I don't believe in capital punishment," he added as the train began to slow. "How can one sentence another man to death?"

"I'm sorry?" Lacey was startled.

"We don't know what death means, do we? How can we impose a punishment we don't understand? You're heading out west, aren't you? Good morning."

The brigadier opened the carriage door and set off. He was clear of the station before his own words on capital punishment began to trouble him. Brigadier Murray-Strachan couldn't remember where he'd heard that argument. On television, probably. It was not something he believed, simply a way of ridding himself of Lacey, and yet the argument troubled him. It was ingenious, too ingenious, it had to have a flaw, which Murray-Strachan couldn't find without giving the matter proper thought.

His car was waiting in a back street near the station and the brigadier watched with sympathy as his sergeant driver fought down the temptation to leap out and open the passenger door. As an unimportant junior, the sergeant was under orders to dress like a civilian, to behave like a civilian and to remain at his post when the brigadier entered the car. But the discipline of the Army was difficult to break and the sergeant needed reminders.

"Stanley," Murray-Strachan said as the car crossed Waterloo Bridge.

"Sir?"

"I thought I asked you to let your hair grow?"

"I left that to the barber, sir."

"Don't have your hair cut short again, Stanley. Do not delegate responsibility to a barber."

"No, sir." Sergeant Stanley didn't sound convnced.

"You're too conspicuous. Only soldiers and recently released convicts wear their hair like that these days."

"Yes, sir."

"I have explained, haven't I, Stanley?"

"Yes, sir. . . . I think so, sir."

"A retired brigadier is not entitled to a sergeant driver."

"No, sir. I understand, sir."

"By all means look like a former soldier, Stanley. But a scruffy former soldier. A time-server, working in ordnance, picking up a redundant brigadier who has fiddled his way back into a soft job which some female Army clerk could do. You with me?"

"Sir."

"And if you wore a sloppy jacket, a loose one, your automatic wouldn't bulge."

"No, sir." Sergeant Stanley was hurt and the brigadier tried to make amends.

"You're an excellent bodyguard, Stanley. But we must blur the image a little. A changing army creates different demands."

"Sir."

"And, oh, I'm thinking of having a dog, Stanley."

"A dog, sir?" Sergeant Stanley was startled.

"A properly trained animal from the Army dog school. A Weimaraner, probably. Looks so innocent to the uninformed, you see? Almost cuddly."

"I'm with you, sir."

"With the live-in gardener the Army has so thoughtfully provided, it should simplify security at my home."

"Thank you, sir." Sergeant Stanley had been troubled by the brigadier's unprotected home. "I'm glad, sir."

"Good. Now Mister Sleet, the American gentleman."

"Sir?"

"When he arrives at the War Office, show him up."

"Yes, sir."

"And do it casually, won't you? He hasn't committed a military crime. Don't march him in."

"No, sir." As the sergeant suppressed his grin, Murray-Strachan smiled into the driving mirror. He liked to put people at their ease, a worried man was inefficient.

But Stanley took the wrong route, they were held up in the traffic and the brigadier became impatient, an emotion he rarely knew. Then the War Office depressed him. The place was so damned shabby, all those temporary offices and aging messengers. The War Office always looked as if an indecisive battle had been fought there the night before. The very building was a strong argument for total peace.

5

MIDDLEMASS REACHED LONDON by devious routes an hour after the brigadier. As his hired car followed the narrow suburban lanes of Surrey from Gatwick Airport, making shadowing difficult, he was drowsing, badly in need of sleep. Drunken Australian dentists had sung their way across the Atlantic, hardly even pausing to watch and wonder at the dawn. He was asleep when the car reached London, dreaming of Doctor Gellner aborting Shona and he started as his driver pulled into the curb.

They were in Knightsbridge and the driver was pointing to the side entrance of Harrods. Middlemass came to swiftly, he had been hunted too early in life to cling to sleep when it was time to act. As he entered Harrods, he realised that the driver of the car had not spoken all the way from Gatwick; he had been as silently efficient as the Sultan of Doha's personal slaves, who had their tongues torn out to prevent needless chatter. Middlemass forced down his fierce hatred of the Sultan, the hatred that must never be allowed to show. Instead he concentrated on crossing Harrods as if it were his friendly neighbourhood store and headed for the Knightsbridge underground station with the exact fare in his hand. He took the Piccadilly line to Green Park, changed to the Victoria line, then took an almost empty District Line train at Victoria.

His man, Harry Walters was waiting in the snack bar by the exit of the Temple underground station and he left as Middlemass went to the counter. By then the financier was bored with the melodrama of Walters' arrangements, but he liked Walters and felt obliged to carry out his part of the charade. Before he followed on, Middlemass ordered a glass of milk and watched the beggars, tramps and derelicts standing in line for their free tea and sandwich, served by the charity worker in the Silver Lady meals-on-wheels wagon parked just beside the snack bar. He noticed that some of this legion of the lost were surprisingly young. One of the youngest and fittest carried a beggar's tray with matchboxes and shoelaces. Middlemass couldn't understand how he could have fallen so low. The beggar didn't look like a junkie, nor did he have the pallor of a convict just out of jail. . . .

He was wasting time so he left the snack bar and walked casually into the Inner Temple, the holy shrine of well-heeled lawyers, where divorces were lied about and cried about and talked into the night about. His feet were heavier than the conscience of that place, he was glad to see Walters sitting by the pond in the middle of the Temple.

"Good to see you at last," he said, but irony was wasted on Walters so he opened his bag and handed over the contracts for closing the oil deal—the documents for Doha, for Zurich and Osaka.

"Thank you, sir." Walters transferred the papers to his coat. "Would you like me to go over my instructions again?"

"I can't wait." Middlemass leaned forward, his head in his hands and closed his weary eyes.

"I hand them over to the courier from Zurich."

"And when will he arrive?"

"Tomorrow, sir."

"Where and when?" Again Walters passed the test.

"My emergency transmitter and the other equipment?"

"In a cabin trunk, sir. Sent on to Rookwood to await your arrival."

"Well done, Walters." The English idiom returned easily.

On an earlier London trip Middlemass had been intrigued by a trial. The short newspaper stories were enough to take him to the court where Harry Walters, then known as Harry Brown, was accused of stealing worthless papers from an office and photographing them before he returned them to the office safe.

Throughout, the defendant maintained he'd stolen the papers for "fun" and he was discharged because he seemed to be without a motive.

But Middlemass' own motives were often equally obscure and he interrogated the man much harder than the prosecution. Walters, or Brown, lived a rich secret life, planning robberies and escapes on obsessionally detailed routes, which began on the underground and ended in Brazil—thousands of miles from his job, his semidetached home in Dracula Gothic, his garden of bindweed and his wife. When he was satisfied, Middlemass offered him a new job and a new name. His London staff was skeletal, a man for the routine work and a press officer whose job was to keep Middlemass' name *out* of the papers, and they knew better than to ask questions when Walters joined them. He had planned the local details of the Doha operation. He was ignorant of everything beyond his minor role, but he knew more than any other man in England.

"Sure we're not being watched?" Middlemass asked, although he knew Walters had no sense of humour.

"Oh, no, sir. This is the *Temple*, sir. No learned gentleman here would allow a stranger to stand by his window."

"Good. And the detailed arrangements?"

"All in the bag I'm leaving on the seat, sir. When I go, lift it and pretend to follow me with it."

"*Pretend* to follow you?"

"Yes, sir. You leave the Temple by the Tudor Street exit then you walk up Bouverie Street and take a taxi to Waterloo Station."

"Take a *cab*? Not the underground?" Middlemass was enjoying himself. In the past, before Harry Walters became involved in genuine intrigue, he had perfected his knowledge of the underground by acting as the Robin Hood of London transport. With mathematical genius and lightning changes he had cheated the underground of pennies, then given the money to the beggars at the station exits. . . .

The young bearded beggar Middlemass had seen at the Silver Lady charity wagon was sitting on the far side of the pond. He was eating the last of his bread by the sign that read DO NOT FEED THE FISH.

"If you go reasonably quickly, you'll catch the next train to Tolchester," Walters said.

"No station at Rookwood now?"

"It isn't used anymore. That's all in the instructions . . . the advice note, I mean. You should get lunch on the train."

"I'm not hungry but I could sure use some sleep," Middlemass said. "Anything more?"

As Walters turned to face him, Middlemass looked into the shapeless grey face and watery blue eyes. Or were the eyes grey, too? Only an artist with a tenacious memory could have reconstructed that face with a drawing or an Identikit set. "There *is* something?"

"Something quite unexpected, sir."

"Unexpected?" Middlemass believed Harry Walters had

prepared for everything but earthquakes and other acts of god. "Talk louder, forget about the beggar," he said. "He'd need exceptional hearing."

"Your daughter, sir. She phoned the office to say she was coming over."

"Oh, no."

"I'm afraid so, sir. Luckily I answered the phone myself."

Middlemass tried to think straight, but he was very tired now and suffering from an unusual clash of emotions. Although he had ordered her to stay in New York, he was proud of her initiative.

"I told her you were staying in London, sir. I didn't know where. You'd changed your mind about Rookwood." Walters didn't sound confident. Shona had apparently convinced him she was as determined as her father.

"But she came and collected the car, sir."

"The Ford?"

"Yes, sir. It had just turned up from Dagenham."

"Let us pray," Middlemass said.

"Yes, sir."

"And stay out of sight until the courier shows up."

"Yes, sir."

"No phone calls to me."

"No, sir. You'll remember to check if the Rookwood telephone's tapped?"

"Yes," Middlemass said. Walters had planned against the most improbable contingencies. "You'll keep in touch as we arranged?"

"Sir," Walters said, "In that bag, you know? How to reach me at any time . . ."

"Yes. Good luck." As Middlemass dismissed him, Walters walked away. He was small and his old-fashioned coat reached almost to his ankles.

Middlemass watched him out of sight, picked up the bag and followed him. But he had not learned his lesson on the Inner Temple as he had on Harrods or the underground and he lost his way. When he turned back, he saw the young beggar behind him, with his tray hidden under his ragged coat. Middlemass stopped by the inscription on the Temple church and read it three times. Then he deliberately wandered, and still the beggar was in sight.

Middlemass stopped a young lawyer with his sack of books, asked the way then walked quickly toward the Tudor Street exit. Still the young beggar was behind him. By then he was sure his imagination wasn't playing tricks. Walters didn't know it all. Maybe he hadn't realised he could also be tailed. Somehow the opposition had found out about Walters and decided he was worth watching. In the process of shrimping they had almost caught the shark. . . .

Almost.

Middlemass walked up to the commissionaire at the gates of the Temple, noted his height, his campaign ribbons and the waxed ends of his moustache, then took a chance.

"You were a Guardsman, weren't you?" he asked hopefully. The rest of the British Army hate the Guards and a retired infantry sergeant would not thank Middlemass for calling him a woodentop.

"Yes, sir. A Coldstreamer, sir. How did you know?"

"Luck." Middlemass said. "I was in a Commando." The truth was sometimes useful.

The commissionaire inspected Middlemass's transatlantic suit. "Commando, were you? You mean an American Ranger?"

"No, Commando."

"Marine Commando, I suppose?" From a Guardsman this was an insult and Middlemass was quick to correct him.

"British Army commando. The Nineteenth."

"The Nineteenth Commando? Were you now? What was your commanding officer called?"

Middlemass told him but the commissionaire wasn't impressed. "Never heard of him, sir, begging your pardon."

"Maybe not. He was killed at Caen."

The commissionaire nodded casually and began to guide a lawyer's car through the iron gates. Middlemass checked on the loitering beggar then made his last attempt. In a tone-deaf bass, he sang the first few bars of the Coldstreamers March. *" 'By the left, by the right, by the centre . . .' "*

The commissionaire obliged with the next stanza . . . *" 'May the cheeks of your arse never fester.' "* So you *were* in the Nineteenth Commando? Didn't know they had any foreigners. I mean no offence, you understand? Anything I can do for you, sir?"

"Well, no, but I respect this place," Middlemass said. "And there's a young beggar over there. He's been selling matches and shoelaces."

"Selling from a tray in the Temple? Excuse me, sir." As he closed on the beggar, Middlemass heard the American accent.

He ambled down Tudor Street, turned into Bouverie Street then walked fast. As he turned into the main thoroughfare of Fleet Street, there was no cab in sight. So Middlemass jumped on the first bus for Waterloo, an artistic flourish Walters might have liked.

On top of the double-decker bus he wondered how Walters' cover had been broken and how and when to warn him. When the West Indian bus conductor stopped beside him, Middlemass automatically held out two coins and asked for Waterloo. He was too preoccupied to look at the coins in his hand.

"You know what you got there, man?" the West Indian

51

conductor asked. "Two fifty pieces. One whole *pound*. Don't do that again, man, not in this city."

"No, I won't. Thank you." Middlemass was troubled by his error and his suddenly ill-organised mind. The filthy version of the Coldstreamers' march, useful as it was, had been something he had discarded from his memory thirty years before with the Nineteenth Commando. . . .

The West Indian conductor was leaning over him talking softly. "I meant what I said, man. You don't want to take chances. Don't trust the English."

6

"YOU ALL KNOW THE FORM," Brigadier Richard Murray-
Strachan said. "We'll take this conference at the clip and get
out of this coal hole quickly." He hated the War Box conference room, which had been designed as a private cinema.
There were no windows, the air-extraction fan sucked up
nothing except speech, and many a senior officer had slept his
way through an important briefing there. For all that,
Murray-Strachan took the sting from his words by showing
his shining morning face. For one thing, this session was
mandatory, the senior civil servants and the top War Box
brass could not justify their jobs without such conferences.
For another, Murray-Strachan had a message of his own to get
across if the briefing went the right way.

"Any one can chip in with any question at any time or
with any additional information they think important.
"Ready, Derek? Carry on."

His staff major rose and cleared his throat. Major Derek
Timpson was good at briefing people. He spoke distinctly, he
listened respectfully and he had a smile that would have sold
fire extinguishers to arsonists.

"Target's name, John Middlemass," he said. "Born near
Jihlava in Moravia, 1922. The first name we have for him is

Jiri Martinu but that probably was an alias, even then."

"Probably?" An elderly general spoke. "You're not certain?"

"Our information is that he changed his name a number of times when the Germans were after him. Besides, Martinu is often a Jewish name and Middlemass is not Jewish . . . sir."

"You're sure he isn't Jewish?" The elderly general sounded disappointed.

"Certain, sir." Major Timpson consulted his notes for effect. They were held to a board by a bulldog clip, a typical Timpson touch, likely to please old officers who kept their maps like this as subalterns in their distant youth. "Nothing much is known about him before the war. But he joined the Czech underground as a courier in March, 1941, and he was captured by the Gestapo in June '42."

Timpson glanced at Murray-Strachan who waved him on, like a member of a golfing foursome sending through a boring pair of players.

"Middlemass or Martinu escaped from the Germans toward the end of '42 and joined the Czech free forces in England in the same year. In May, 1943, . . ."

"A remarkable escape," the old general said. "Truly miraculous. Not possible, is it, Richard? Not on?"

Murray-Strachan didn't want to argue with his superiors but he had no option. "It happened sometimes, and Middlemass kept in contact with his comrades long after the war. Particularly a German Jewish doctor called Otsch Gellner with a remarkable war record. He's Middlemass' doctor in New York, as it happens. May we carry on, sir?" the brigadier asked.

Major Timpson geared up to 130 words a minute. "Middlemass served with the Free Czech forces for a very short time. But they weren't likely to see action for some time, so he volunteered for the British Army and was dumped in the Pioneer Corps." The Pioneer Corps was a joke force to officers from the fighting arms and Timpson got the audience reaction he wanted.

"No further connection with the Gestapo was ever traced. Therefore, . . ."

"Therefore the fellow was very sharp," the old general said. "Obvious what happened, wasn't it? The Gestapo sent him over here as a spy. Then he saw how the war was going and decided to get back on the winning side. Don't you agree, Richard?"

"I really can't be certain, sir," Murray-Strachan said, nodding to Timpson, who did his best to speed up his delivery.

"Therefore, . . ." Timpson said, "Martinu or Middlemass was transferred to a young soldiers' training battalion in Northern Ireland. He was commissioned at Barnard Castle in . . ."

"In the British Army?" The old general was scandalised.

"Yes, sir. In the Moray Rifles, sir. Then he transferred to the Nineteenth Commando, where he won the Distinguished Service Order. . . ."

"As a subaltern?" the old general asked. "Unusual."

"Doesn't apply, sir. Middlemass was a troop commander. He reached field rank in . . ."

"We had Middlemass as a major in the Nineteenth Commando?"

"Yes, sir. After the war he served with the War Crimes Commission, Court 101, Curio Haus, Hamburg. He had a gift for languages and . . ."

"Just a moment." The elderly general would not be rushed. "Don't we have anything on his black-market fiddles in Hamburg at the time? Place was wide open for confidence tricksters. And he was a Commando, after all. Special Forces

55

were full of tricky people like him. Am I right, Richard?"

"Of course, sir." Murray-Strachan had spent his war behind the Japanese lines with Special Force 136.

"Well, then?"

"Just coming to that, sir," Major Timpson said. "In September of 1945, Middlemass got himself demobilised and joined the civilian show, the British Control Commission for Germany. That was in Münster. Then he vanished for a time."

The old general folded his arms and sat back, satisfied.

"In the same year he reappeared at British Army headquarters at Bad Oeynhausen."

"Hardly surprising." The general was content, staring at the acoustic tiles on the ceiling. "One could get anything in Bad Oeynhausen, couldn't one, Richard?"

"No idea, sir."

"Oh, come along. A bit of frat, a fraulein for a bar of chocolate. Surely you remember?"

"No, sir. I was in the east at the time. Carry on, will you, Derek?"

"In the same year he reappeared at Bad Oeynhausen. As the papal emissary or whatever."

"As the what?" Vincent Connor asked the question. He was the senior civil servant, the most important man in the room.

"As the papal emissary, Mister Connor," Major Timpson said. "Perhaps Colonel Padre Radford might . . ." He looked for help to Padre David Radford, the only chaplain in intelligence, but Radford did not appear to hear.

"Go on. Do go on," Vincent Connor said.

"Well, he had a chitty or a bull or whatever one gets from the Pope. So the Army set him up in rather a grand style and gave him a staff so that he could organise Red Cross trains to evacuate the needy Catholic sick to Holy Belgium.''

Timpson consulted the notes he didn't need, intimidated by Connor's hostile stare. At last he took courage and looked up. "You're not a Catholic, are you, sir?"

"Don't let it trouble you," Vincent Connor said.

"Truly sorry, Mister Connor," Timpson said. "Middle-mass' papers were forged, of course. He wasn't even a Catholic."

"Orthodox, I expect," the old general said and waited for the answer that did not come. "Padre?"

Padre Radford ignored him.

"Colonel Radford, I asked you a question."

"I'm sorry, sir." Padre Radford rose. He was unusually tall and spectacularly bald. No one knew why a priest should be serving with intelligence. When he was asked, Colonel Padre Radford evaded the question. "I'm not an authority on the various sects of Czechoslovakia, *sir*." Radford sat down, indicating that the subject was closed. As a padre, he could risk showing his contempt for fools of any rank.

Murray-Strachan gestured to Timpson to cover the awkward pause. "Middlemass knew that the Belgians badly needed thermometers and that the Germans were desperate for cigarettes. So he bought thermometers in Germany at one cigarette each and sold them in Belgium for cigarettes. Each thermometer was worth the equivalent in tobacco of a hundred cigarettes."

A murmur of distaste ran round the room surprising Murray-Strachan. Had they forgotten how European refugees had hated the Germans?

"I hardly need tell you that Middlemass was filling the mattresses beneath the sick with thermometers in Germany, exchanging them in Belgium and filling the mattresses with tobacco on their way back," Timpson said.

"Anyone care to try to calculate the profit ratio?" Vincent Connor asked. He was looking at Colonel Radford, his fellow intellectual.

"Geometrical progression," Radford said. "Not my line, I fear. Perhaps someone in logistics . . ."

"And he was never caught?" The old general interrupted quickly before they strayed toward such rubbish as logistics.

"No, sir," Major Timpson said. "Middlemass left Bad Oeynhausen before a single train was searched. But the Special Investigation Branch found that his papers were forged." He was talking for the benefit of Connor, the religious civilian. "The whole thing was kept quiet, naturally. We apologised to the Vatican as a matter of form." Timpson was a practising Anglican, with no desire to offend a Roman.

"And the whole of the Army Special Investigation Branch couldn't hound him down?" the old general asked.

"No, sir. They had no idea at the time that it was Middlemass and we've had no proof since. Besides he'd vanished completely. He reappeared in the American occupied zone of Germany as a very wealthy man and he married a rather rich American Army nurse."

"Very stoutly shod," Murray-Strachan murmured. "Avril Bergen of the Wall Street banking family."

"So he wormed his way across the Atlantic?" the general asked, and Murray-Strachan nodded, hiding his distress at the general's ugly choice of words. "Then he moved in on the family bank, I suppose?"

"No, sir," the brigadier said. For once, he was pleased by the interruption. It was time they understood Middlemass was a loner. "He set up for himself as a speculator, then an investment banker. I think they call it. He's rather richer than his wife's relatives now."

"Can't say I've ever heard of him," the old general said. "I know of the Bergens, of course."

"Middlemass goes out of his way to keep his name out of the papers," Murray-Strachan said. "He prefers to be known only to the people he deals with." He gazed apologetically at his spokesman but he had to get on. They were overrunning conference time and he still had to place a larger commercial in some natural break somewhere.

"The map, sir?" Major Timpson asked.

"The map," Murray-Strachan replied and the map of the Middle East oil reserves appeared on the screen. Shaded areas showed where the military situation was particularly unstable and where Anglo-American oil interests were threatened.

"I understand the shading." Vincent Connor's nasal voice rose, he sounded testy. "But what is the significance of the numbers in yellow?" More than ever, the senior civil servant looked as if he had a bad smell directly under his nose. Timpson retreated in good order by turning toward the brigadier.

"The yellow figures?" Murray-Strachan repeated. "They show the amounts in millions of dollars the CIA have spent in troubled areas on bribery. . . . Sorry, sir, I mean persuasion. Sweetening local sheikhs and so on. Even crossing the rather bloody palms of terrorists from time to time. If you will look at the Persian-Russian frontier . . ."

"I have no desire to look at Iran or Russia," Mister Connor said. "I don't know where you got those figures and I don't wish to know. Brigadier Murray-Strachan?"

"Sir?"

"I'd like the yellow numbers erased from that map. We

have not been at war with the United States of America for some considerable time."

"No, sir. Quite so. But the yellow figures are significant. May I explain?" He took the civilian's silence for assent. "If you will look at the figures again, you will see that the American government has spent more money on—eh—enticement in the Sultanate of Doha than in any other oil-producing area of the Middle East."

Vincent Connor nodded abruptly. Normally he was a man of measured movements and a jerk from this civilian was sufficient warning for most staff officers concerned with their careers. Murray-Strachan chose to ignore it.

"Despite that, Mr. Middlemass has been allowed to become the friend and confidant of the Sultan of Doha," the brigadier said. "This investment banker has become adviser to the most reactionary Arab leader since Ibn Saud."

"Indeed," the civil servant said. "But this happened at a time when the United States government had no reason to distrust Middlemass."

"We must agree to differ on that point," the brigadier said. "I am simply trying to establish that Middlemass is a very smooth operator." He was trying to establish more than that and he knew that Connor was not fooled. Just then a staff captain knocked, entered and drew Major Timpson's attention. Timpson went out. Normally Murray-Strachan disliked such interruptions but this one could not have been better timed.

"No one seemed to worry when Middlemass bought a subsidiary drilling company and let it be known that he intended to drill for water in Doha."

"Why not?" Vincent Connor was no longer testy, there was a hint of menace in his voice. "In certain parts of Doha, water is scarcer than oil."

Murray-Strachan thanked him for this obvious informa-

60

tion. "Padre," he said to Colonel Radford, "I wonder if you could carry on from there? Major Timpson appears to have a more pressing appointment."

As the nervous titter subsided, Padre Radford strolled to the rostrum. He took the pointer and gazed round languidly, like a headmaster about to address a captive audience of schoolboys.

"Middlemass found his proving oil wells here and here. One onshore, as you can see. The other is offshore. I mention that in case any of you should be colour blind. He found the oil at a cost of two or three million dollars. Then he set off to prove the extent of the field and that must have cost him between eighty and ninety million dollars."

"Is this information essential?" Vincent Connor asked.

"*We* think so, *sir*," Murray-Strachan said. "Would you be kind enough to bear with us for a moment?" The brigadier knew that Connor was a dedicated man and that the Minister of Defence leaned on him like a crutch. But he felt that Connor lacked subtlety. Murray-Strachan was equally dedicated; he held that the ruling class of any nation loses control when it loses its belief in itself and its purpose. But he had discovered as a young officer that the British are deeply suspicious of purposeful, intelligent men and he had learned to cloak his intent, his ambition and his ability by appearing slothful here, cynical there or rule-bound and dogmatic as the moment and the mood demanded. He was pleased that Vincent Connor hadn't learned the same lesson. He was walking into the trap Murray-Strachan had prepared for him. . . .

"I will bear with you for a *moment*," Connor said.

"Thank you, Padre? Can we have the oil figures now? What our western allies would call the yawn factor, so I'm told."

"In Doha, Middlemass ended with a true put of a quarter of a million barrels of oil a day," Padre Radford said. "High quality, sulphur-free oil. If the estimate is right, the potential of the Doha oil field is three and a half million barrels a day." Murray-Strachan recognised the special note in that voice. Padre Radford was mocking the members of the conference. He had asked to be excused from the session. Now he was delivering statistics in an organloft bray like a more conventional Army chaplain at a drumhead service. One day Radford's intellectual snobbery would undo him and the brigadier hoped that day would soon dawn.

"You take the point?" Murray-Strachan asked Connor.

"I don't require a sermon on the subject," Connor said. "We are being reminded, aren't we, that Doha is the only major oil-producing nation in the Middle East with an uninterrupted passage of oil to deep-water ports in the Indian Ocean?

Padre Radford leaned on the pointer which was just tall enough to support him, a quarter staff for Little John. "When Middlemass made his strike, the oil companies of the West could do nothing other than wait until he offered them his oil. And he did nothing of the kind. It became all too clear that Middlemass could impose his own price . . . or control the posted price if you prefer the oily boys' jargon. If he so desired, he could break the oil monopolies of the Middle East, do what the Russians have tried so often without significant success."

"Where do the Russians come in?" The old general sounded irritable, Murray-Strachan had hoped he'd be asleep by then.

"The Russians have their own oil, sir." Murray-Strachan cut in before Padre Radford could be rude. "But they like to buy in the Middle East then undersell the Americans or the British to keep the situation unstable."

"I see," the old general said and he didn't.

"But Middlemass didn't do that," Murray-Strachan said.

"Is this a guessing game, Richard?" the general asked.

"No, sir. It's now quite clear that Middlemass intends to sell his oil to the Japanese. At no greater price than the Americans would be forced to pay. Probably less than the Germans, who are rather desperate for a stake in Middle Eastern oil fields . . . almost as desperate as the Japanese. You probably know that all oil sources will be exhausted within thirty years, if we continue to use it at our present rate."

The elderly general blew his nose. It was something of a bugle call for a minute's silence while he thought. "Now look here," the general said at last, "the Japanese fought a war to get the oil of the Far East. They lost the war but they've won the peace and they've got all that Far Eastern oil sewn up. Why should they worry about the Middle East?"

Murray-Strachan kept his face averted, in case his elation showed. The conference was going better than he had dared to hope, he couldn't have guessed that the old general would prove such an excellent straight man. "I know it's not your field, sir," he said, "but the Indonesian oil wells are the only significant ones left in the Far East. They're running out, sir, and they supply less than ten percent of Japan's oil now. By 1980 the Japanese might want to consume eighty percent of the world's total supply of oil, sir. And the main commercial reserves for all the world are in the Middle East."

"I see." Again the general paused for thought. "But the military reserves are in Alaska and the North Sea and so on, aren't they?"

"Yes, sir. The strategic reserves are there, for the moment."

"Precisely. So how does it come about that this Middlemass

affair is a military matter? It's a civilian problem, surely? And it should be handled by the civvy cloak-and-dagger chaps. Don't you agree?"

"I'm not permitted to have an opinion on that subject, sir," Murray-Strachan said and the dimmest members of the audience took his point.

"Leave that to the Minister, if you please." Vincent Connor made no attempt to cloak his order in courtesy or to obey the normal rules of procedure.

"I'm sorry?" Murray-Strachan asked. He rather liked that phrase, he'd picked it up from that fool Lacey on the train.

"I think you understood me. Political and economic matters are the Minister's province."

"Now, just a minute, Connor," the old general said. "If I understand him correctly, Richard Murray-Strachan would be more than pleased to leave the whole thing to the politicians and their people. That's the point he's making, don't you see?"

As Connor and the old general battled it out as the best-of-a-three-stares wrestling match, Murray-Strachan decided to move on. He had placed his commercial and he had always argued that there was no such thing as objective truth. He gave the rest of the facts as he saw them.

"Despite the amount of largesse that the Americans have distributed," he said, "Middlemass has convinced the Sultan that the American government is Doha's enemy. And that the Americans intend to promote civil disorder and foment a revolt so that they can take over all his oil at bargain-basement prices."

"Oversimplified," Connor said.

"Perhaps, sir, but we're overrunning time. Middlemass has

friends in high places in the United States and we do not know who they are or why they've helped him. Or his own motives for that matter. If the Americans removed Middlemass, the Sultan would be certain that his dead friend had been telling the truth and the Sultan would no doubt sell to the Japanese himself. . . ." Vincent Connor was looking at his watch although the clock was on his eyeline.

"So Middlemass has to be taken out in England," Murray-Strachan said. "And his demise has to look like an accident, the kind of accident that the Sultan of Doha will understand and believe."

When Connor rose and studiedly put his papers in his briefcase, the brigadier appeared to take his cue.

"Any further questions, gentlemen?" he asked. "The actual plan of the operation will be discussed later. By the way, the name for the operation is Bullterrier."

"Nasty bloody creatures, can't think why anyone breeds them," the old general muttered. "Why Bullterrier, may I ask?"

"As you know, sir, a properly trained guarding bullterrior will wag its tail as a marauder enters and let him pass inside the house. Then it holds him there. And if he tries to leave, the bullterrier will go for his throat . . . or some other delicate area."

"Did you think of that code name, Richard?" the general asked.

"No, sir."

"Not surprised. The name and the whole damned operation smacks of clever-clever civilians. I don't see how it concerns the Army at all."

The old general rose and left the room. He was known for his iron whim and his rusty bladder. As his juniors gathered their notes and followed him, the civil servants left in a body, using the other door. But Connor stayed behind. He had begun the winding-up ceremony but he was still arranging the papers in his briefcase.

"Considering an early retirement, Richard?" Vincent Connor asked.

"No, I'm not."

"Then why did you manipulate your audience in that outrageous fashion?"

"Manipulate it?"

Connor sighed. "It has been decided at the highest level that this is a matter for military intelligence. So it's your pigeon."

"So I understand."

"But you spent the conference making it clear you wanted no part in the operation. May I ask why?"

Murray-Strachan locked his briefcase and put the key on the chain in his pocket. "Can I be frank, sir?"

"My dear fellow, you've been more than frank all morning but I doubt if you're being frank now. You don't normally call me 'sir' in private."

"Sorry, force of habit. My orders were to pretend that the operation has not yet been planned in detail, although you and I know that it has. I'm forbidden to tell any of my staff that a junior British officer is to be used as bait. Nor that Radford is reporting to you directly."

"The junior officer troubles you, Richard?"

"Very much. He'll trouble the whole Army."

"Not unless it becomes public knowledge, *Richard*."

"Not *until* it becomes public knowledge, *Vincent*. Such things have a nasty habit of bobbing up."

"So you're covering yourself in advance?"

"Don't think I follow you." Murray-Strachan nodded formally and walked out.

He had taken five paces when Colonel Radford opened the door of the projection room and gestured. Major Timpson was sitting inside and Radford closed the projection room door behind them.

"All right, tell him," he said.

"The Americans, sir. They're moving in on our parish." Murray-Strachan was too surprised to answer.

"Do they know Middlemass is heading for Rookwood, sir?"

"I shouldn't think so." Murray-Strachan had found out about Rookwood and he was proud of his fieldwork. He had been in touch with most of Middlemass's British associates, since he was a member of most of the right clubs. By perseverance and a bit of luck, he had tracked down Laurence Adam, who was to be Middlemass's host.

"No, I don't suppose they could know about Rookwood. But Sleet phoned you this morning and told you that the target had arrived?"

"Yes."

"Well, sir, that means they had their own men at Gatwick."

"Everyone has resident spies at Gatwick," Murray-Strachan said. "Even the Albanians, I imagine. I was rather amused when Sleet chose to tell me, though."

"And now they've got a tail on Harris Walters, Middlemass's London contact."

"Oh, my God."

"And Walters led the tail to Middlemass. An idiot with a beard masquerading as a beggar followed him through the Inner Temple."

Murray-Strachan was so annoyed he overwound the watch that had once belonged to his father.

"Middlemass spotted him, no doubt?"

"Of course, sir."

"Thank you, gentlemen," Murray-Strachan said. "I must have words with Mr. Sleet."

7

"Coffee?" Brigadier Murray-Strachan asked his American visitor.

"No thanks." Matthew Sleet drew the line at British coffee. He was a large, fat man, normally expressionless, he conveyed shades of meaning with polite, formalised gestures.

"Tea?"

"Nothing thanks."

"Warm enough?" Murray-Strachan asked. Sleet smiled, he was apparently impervious to cold, he could even survive in a lightweight suit in the War Box.

"Very comfortable," Sleet said. "Nice place you've got here. Homey." The brigadier's office was as cold and white and monastic as he meant it to be. There was not a picture, a map, a lamp or even an obtrusive ashtray to distract attention.

"I thought you'd like it," Murray-Strachan said, joining the act as usual. "You look absolutely right for this room with your tropical suit and your desert boots. *Desert* boots? Isn't that rather un-American?"

"I'm trying to blend with the natives," Sleet said. "Didn't one of your Cabinet ministers wear suede boots? *Purple* suede?"

"Perhaps that's why he's no longer in office," Murray-Strachan said. "Pity in a way. I don't think he'd have bought this operation. Quite honestly I don't."

Sleet yawned. "Come on," he said. "We exchange eliminations. Murders without obvious motives or suspects. You do one for us, we do one for you. The authorised version of *Strangers on a Train*."

"Hitchcock," Murray-Strachan said. "Rather apt. Hitch and cock."

His telephone rang. Murray-Strachan listened, said, "Good," and replaced the receiver.

"We can't help the hitch," Sleet said. "Middlemass has a very powerful weapon. He can't be eliminated until certain . . . false evidence has been destroyed."

"Blackmail?" Murray-Strachan talked as if he hadn't considered the possibility. "Obviously he has powerful friends in the State Department but . . ."

"His powerful friends aren't working for him now."

"Then may I know what the blackmail is about?"

"It concerns the President and it won't help."

"If it concerns the President, I'd rather not know." Murray-Strachan spoke unusually swiftly. "You realise, of course, that the extra time will mean extra men? And that we're rather understaffed?"

When he smiled, genuinely, Sleet imposed an image of boyhood on his impassive face. "Don't think I don't sympathise," he said. "You don't have too many good men in the field, now that the James Bond vein's worked out. I noticed that, way back in Berlin."

"Quite so," Murray-Strachan said. "And you had so many men falling over one another that they didn't even notice that the Berlin Wall was being built." There was no sting in his remark, they both knew that Sleet owed his promotion to the shambles of American intelligence in Berlin.

For all that Sleet cupped his ear. "Do I detect an edge?" he asked. "Have your senior generals been getting to you?"

"They have, indeed," Murray-Strachan said. "For some reason they don't think I want this particular operation. It's not really an Army job, of course."

"That puzzles me, too," Sleet said. "Why *is* it an Army job? My outfit's civilian, after all."

Murray-Strachan listened with admiration. Sleet reminded him of that chap crossing a room, his eyes ablaze with insincerity. "I *have* heard it suggested that you asked for me," Murray-Strachan said. "But you couldn't have, could you? Not an old friend?" The brigadier wondered if Sleet would go on smiling if he knew the full plan as it had been dreamed up by Murray-Strachan's masters.

"Let's go over the salient points again," Murray-Strachan said. "We have to remove Middlemass before he sells his oil to the Japanese. But not before you give the word."

"Correct."

"Then, we have to be sure that the killing can't be traced to any American agency," the brigadier said. "Thirdly, we have to convince the Sultan of Doha that Middlemass's death was an unfortunate accident." Sleet nodded. "Fourthly, we have to block the inevitable public curiosity in England and the States until you've reawakened the Sultan's love sufficiently to get your hands on his oil." He was searching through his desk. He found an almost empty tin of throat pastilles and offered it to Sleet as an ashtray. "Or should we say *our* hands?" the brigadier asked. "I believe that some understanding has been reached by the American and British oil empires. I hope so."

"How long do you figure we'll keep the newspapers muzzled?" Sleet asked. "The reporters will go on digging till they come up with something. A month maybe?"

"Longer with any luck," Murray-Strachan said. "Then we'll have to provide them with a few juicy bones. Buried, of course. But not too deeply. With all the clues placed where fearless journalists can find them."

"That's worked, once," Sleet said. "But will it always work?"

"I'm not clairvoyant," Murray-Strachan said. "But my masters' theory is that one of your newshounds or one of ours will find out who killed Middlemass. This killer will have a sufficiently bizarre past and a convincingly improbable motive for the newspapers to accept it. As in the case of Commander Crabb. As in the Philby affair."

Sleet was grinning. "You can play the stiff-assed British brigadier so well you had me fooled for years, he said. "Sometimes you even fool yourself. But when the mood hits you, you've got a mind like one of the Borgias."

"Not me, dear fellow, my employers. And the Borgias had motives. What, precisely, is Middlemass's motive?"

"We're working on that," Sleet said.

"Good. My masters want this situation tidied up quickly. Perhaps that's why they've taken so little time and trouble over their plan."

"I don't know about that," Sleet said. "You've had some damn wild spies in England. Not a decent motive between them but you were believed and you got them jailed."

"We've done our best," Murray-Strachan said. "But we've never been in your class."

"You don't mean that?"

"I do," the brigadier said. "For implausible assassins with the most outrageous motives, the United States' record is second to none. One inconvenient messiah after another has left the world stage a trifle hurriedly. And every new assassin sounds less likely than the last."

Sleet, for once, was not amused. He walked to the window and stared out on Whitehall and the Cenotaph. As the brigadier waited, he could hear Sleet faintly whistling *The Colonel Bogey March.*

"All right," Sleet said, "I've caught your act before and you've caught mine. If I call it quits now, if I turn up the applause machine, will you tell me what you're planning?"

"What my masters are planning." Murray-Strachan said. "We understand that Middlemass will be staying on the Hampshire-Dorset border."

"That so?"

"So we can lay on a hunting accident," Murray-Strachan said.

"A shooting accident?"

"Not as you understand it," the brigadier said. "The first chap to be suspected will be a nice fellow who was only aiming to take home a brace of pheasants."

Sleet kept staring at the window although the light had almost gone. "It could be," he said, doubtfully. "A hunting accident's the kind of thing the Sultan of Doha might just buy. He's always after oryx."

Murray-Strachan was playing with his paper clips, arranging them in threes in column of march. "The story *might* stand the test of months . . . if we can be certain there are no Americans in the neighbourhood."

"I can vouch for my people," Sleet said, "no interference." He was reluctant to talk about the rival American outfit, which had sent their own men. It was typical of the President to set men against men and agencies against agencies. Sleet

73

had to admit that the President had never equalled Stalin's feat of pitting two of his marshals and two of his armies against each other, to capture one German city. But the President hadn't had the same temptations, yet. . . .

"Thinking, are you?" Murray-Strachan asked. "Supposing the Middlemass killer happens to be an Army officer? Then the reporters establish that he joined our Army as a member of a revolutionary cadre?"

Sleet stubbed out his cigarette in the lozenge tin and ground it until it burst. "I thought you didn't watch imported TV series. Revolutionary cadres in the Army? Isn't that kinda dated? Jane Fonda was a one-star general in that outfit."

"Bear with me," Murray-Strachan said. "Not only has this young British officer been a revolutionary. On service in Arabia he was responsible for the death of a loyal sergeant major."

Sleet was already reaching for another cigarette. "That's British TV," he said. "We never stoop that low."

Murray-Strachan took a bottle and two glasses from the steel filing cabinet marked MOST SECRET. "Someone worked rather hard on this idea. If you don't like it, I can pass it back."

Sleet shook his head. "I'm not foolish enough to let you back down. The British Army won't buy this story, but who cares?"

Murray-Strachan locked his fingers and rested his chin on his hands as if in prayer. "I care," he said. "But this assassin could be useful once he's as dead as Middlemass. The poor young anarchist will be committing suicide, of course, just before the newspapers get to him."

"Naturally," Sleet said. "How could he live with himself?"

"The whole affair will be exposed by the media," the brigadier said. "Obviously the Army will deny it. But in the corridors of Whitehall, we will apologise for our incredible error in recruiting such a man." He was warned by Sleet's lowered eyelids. "In the process the Army can tighten up security and screening. They can weed out all the suspect officers, particularly those who are not wildly enthusiastic about the new role of British infantry."

"The new role of your Army as a political police force?"

"No need to be crude," the brigadier said. "But something of the kind has come about in Ulster."

"I follow you," Sleet said. "Your Army's learning from the French. I even think the Pentagon envies you a little, but I'm not wild about supporting the British colonels."

"No? You helped the Egyptian colonels, practically invented them," Murray-Strachan said. "And the Greek colonels. Possibly even the Libyan colonels, if one of our sources is correct. So why not the British colonels?" He thought his distaste was clear and he was surprised by Sleet's expression.

"Don't misunderstand me," Murray-Strachan said.

"I'm trying not to."

"Try harder," Murray-Strachan said. "The British colonels are no more capable of organising a revolution than the British Communist Party or the Salvation Army. But we mustn't discourage them, must we? I want them to stand up and be counted. Then I can deal with them." Winkling out the fascist colonels was a project dear to Murray-Strachan.

"Are your Army officers going to be dumb enough to believe all that? Sleet asked. "This young revolutionary officer. He's *too* implausible. Somebody's not going to buy this story. Somebody's going to work until they prove that you've invented him."

Murray-Strachan gathered his bowler and his umbrella. "We've been here long enough. Our usual place? It'll be pretty well deserted, I should think."

"Could be," Sleet said. "But I don't think I can drink any more right now. My stomach's in bad shape."

Murray-Strachan had heard that story before. "I think your digestion will function somehow," he said. "I didn't invent this revolutionary subaltern, by the way. He exists, and the Army's been wondering what to do with him. He should be back in Britain shortly."

Sleet watched the brigadier refurling his umbrella. "You're not trying very hard to sell me this idea, are you?" he asked.

"Why should I? It's not a brand of detergent," the brigadier said. "It's a rather filthy product, in fact."

His telephone rang again. The brigadier listened, said, "Even better," then replaced the receiver.

"Matthew, my dear fellow," he said, "we've always been friendly."

"I suspect the worst," Sleet said.

"Weren't you leaving this side of the ocean to us?" the brigadier asked.

"Give it to me straight," Sleet said.

"I didn't mind your resident correspondent at Gatwick announcing that Middlemass was here. But I do mind bearded beggars following our target in the Inner Temple, of all places."

"Is this a joke?"

"I wish it were," Murray-Strachan said. "He was an American, carrying official papers."

Sleet leaned forward. He was so angry that the brigadier wondered if he'd try to hit him. "Listen," Sleet said, "I came down hard and obvious in New York to run Middlemass out.

I even had a hand in that myself. I wanted him to move here. He was clearly moving somewhere and I was worried he'd change his mind and head for Zurich or even Doha. But I haven't got too many men on this side of the Atlantic."

"I'd like to believe you," Murray-Strachan said. "But I must warn you that if your fellows collide with ours, this operation could be a shambles."

"Not my people." Sleet told him the minimum about the rival American agency.

"Pity you hadn't mentioned them before," the brigadier said.

"Where is this agent now?"

"In jail, I fear," Murray-Strachan said.

"In a British *jail*. How?"

"He was caught in possession of dangerous drugs. And now I propose . . ."

"Don't," Sleet said. "Leave the rest to me."

"Are you sure? I imagine we'll have time to spare."

"You won't," Sleet said. "I'm expecting fresh orders tonight. I think Washington's ready to have Middlemass removed now."

"Now?"

"As soon as you're ready," Sleet said, "as soon as it can look accidental."

"Change of heart at the White House?"

"No, I don't think so." Sleet was unwilling to admit the President had changed his mind and decided he had more to lose by letting Middlemass live than by letting the investment banker's letters reach the newspapers. "Not a change of heart. A tighter schedule, that's all."

"I hope it's not too tight," the brigadier said.

8

At Rookwood House, Laurence Adam's housekeeper answered the door. "*Mr.* Middlemass," she said. "We've been so *concerned* about you." Mrs. Phillips was a superior housekeeper and she never used a simple, direct word when a cold and vague one would do. "The chauffeur is waiting for you at Tolchester Station," she said, giving "chauffeur" the full French impact. "The squire is not at home, I fear."

"I got off down the line and took a taxi," Middlemass said. "Sorry to cause so much trouble." He was carrying his bag and he saw her glance toward the taxi, expecting his valet to bring in his golf clubs and his gun cases. As the hired car moved away, Mrs. Phillips looked distrustfully at Middlemass's single bag. He had lived at Rookwood before, he had suffered from her in the past and he remembered she was called Droop Drawers by the locals.

"Haven't my other things arrived?"

"Your trunk? Indeed it has. Supper will be served at . . ."

"I don't want supper, thank you," he said, "I'll have a sandwich now."

"But . . ."

"I don't want to inconvenience you. If it's too much trouble, I'll have a sandwich at the pub."

79

"Your sandwiches will be ready in a moment, sir. I believe there is a fire in the library."

"I'll go and find out for sure," he said. Middlemass thought he had drowned his inverted snobbery on his first westward crossing of the Atlantic. But it still bobbed up when he talked to people like Mrs. Phillips.

The telephone was on the table by the fire of elm logs. Middlemass checked his watch. He wanted to phone the Stafford and contact Shona. As far as he knew, it was the only hotel in London she'd ever used and he did not expect her heightened social conscience would drive her to a cheaper hotel on this side of the ocean.

He lifted the phone, remembered the Stafford's number, then something more. According to Harry Walters, English telephone engineers had a code for every area and the Rookwood code was 352. When they had serviced a telephone, engineers used the code to make sure that the number was ringing out. But the same code could be used for other things. Middlemass dialed 352 then the number on Adam's phone. The result mystified him, he cleared the line and redialled. For the second time there were two distinct clicks before the number started ringing out. If Walters was right, this meant that the phone was tapped through the exchange.

Middlemass sat staring into the fire, thinking it out. He knew that official wire-tapping was almost as common in England as at home but he didn't think the British government would keep an ear on Laurence Adam, who was unimportant and generally considered honest to the point of idiocy. He also knew he might have been spotted at the airport but he couldn't see how Sleet had traced him to Rookwood so quickly. Even if he had, he could never have tapped a line like this, alone. The British might pretend not to know about a button-sized bug in the telephone's mouthpiece placed by a bogus engineer, but they could hardly ignore a heavy tap through their government-owned exchange.

The simple answer was that the British were cooperating with Washington, which didn't surprise or trouble him too much. He had no greater respect for the British than for Sleet. So long as he distracted their attention from Walters and the Zurich courier, the plan still worked. The main thing was to keep them busy until the Zurich courier was safely on his way back.

Middlemass spent hours with the Rookwood maps, committing the tracks to memory until he heard the tyres screech on the gravel.

"What's this supposed to be?" Shona asked him when he followed Mrs. Phillips across the drive to meet the car.

"A car," he said. "A British Ford. I think they call it an estate car but it's quiet and unostentatious. It's a family car, in fact."

"Some family. What have you done to it?" she asked.

"I've got friends at Dagenham and they may have . . . well . . . improved its performance. But it should handle beautifully and it's safe."

"Safe? I put my foot down and took off," she said. "You know I haven't got a pilot's licence."

9

"I wish it was raining," Sergeant Todd said. "Always wanted to come home from Arabia in the rain."

"Give it time," Lieutenant Max Lawson said. "We'll be shoveling snow come November. And if that's all we're shovelling we'll be lucky."

Their airtrooper was circling over English fields, denied permission to land. Out on the edge of the Empty Quarter of Arabia, Max had forgotten that aspect of southern English life. Down below there was a permanent traffic jam and even the air was overcrowded. . . .

Sergeant Todd tapped his platoon commander. "Landing lights, sir," he said.

"Yes," Max replied. While men from an independent parachute patrol company looked down on English homes and English fields with wonder, Max stared at the lifejacket diagram on the bulkhead.

"Thanks," he said, accepting a barley sugar from the stewardess without looking up. She had seemed so desireable when they left Arabia, the flesh-clothed fantasy for most of the men in the platoon. But she was only another woman now they were home. Most of the men didn't bother to thank her as she passed with brushing breasts and barley sugars. They had women of their own in England. Some of them even had wives or girls waiting by the barriers down below. No one was waiting for Max, he hadn't told even his parents that he was coming home. No one would be expecting Sergeant Todd, whose wife had gone off with another man while Todd was sweating it out. . . .

"Cheer up, sir," the sergeant said. "That's England down there, not the arsehole of the empire." He was talking about the independent Arab state of Akdhar, where they'd fought their last action.

"I don't want to wear my smile out too early." Max said. "I'm keeping it for the landing."

"Forget about the sergeant major, sir," Todd said. "He's dead and you didn't kill him."

"Wish I could forget about him," Max said. "How many men do you reckon you've killed?"

"Lost count. I'm not a fucking fighter pilot, sir."

"Me neither," Max said, "so I can't get rid of the sergeant major."

"No? Most of our shower would have chewed the sergeant major's kidneys on toast. One of them got the chance and took it. So what do we do, sniff him out then turn the poor bugger in?"

"It doesn't matter who squeezed the trigger, we're responsible."

"Not now," the sergeant said. "Leave it to Scarface." The military police officer who first investigated the case had a scar across his nose and under one eye, the result of a Land-rover accident. But the scar looked like a sabre fighter's slip and the police officer had worked with a Germanic dedication. "He talked to everybody, one at a time," Todd said. "And they all told the same bedtime story. The sergeant major was killed by an Arab sniper, so they said. Eight of them swore they saw him go down. They've told that story so often that *they* believe it. They'll be telling it to their wives in their bloody sleep. Scarface didn't even call me in."

Max unwrapped the barley sugar, examined it, then dropped it into the waste tray. Why the hell were military transports still handing out sweeties after so many civil airlines had given up?

"He didn't talk to you and he didn't talk to me," Max said. "The rest of the time he was as busy as a bluebottle. You ever heard of a Redcap officer investigating a murder without talking to the platoon commander? Or the sergeant?"

"No," Todd said.

"And the man who shot the sergeant major in the back? Who would he try to blame? Who would he try to nail up?"

"You or me," the sergeant said.

"You *and* me. They wouldn't stand up for an officer or a sergeant. Not in our mob. Not any longer."

The engines faded. They both fitted their safety belts and put their cigarettes out, obeying the regulations at last. Then they sat in silence, listening. They hated flying without parachutes and they knew too much about the stalling speed of the aircraft. Then the engines roared, the nose lifted, the plane began circling again.

"So what do you reckon to do about it, sir?"

"I don't know," Max said. "We missed our chance when the plane landed in Cyprus."

"You weren't thinking of settling there and bottling Cyprus sherry, were you, sir?"

"I'd rather bottle you. We could have gone into hospital.

With a mysterious pain in the skull. Anything they couldn't check on right away. Then we could have nipped out of that hospital and made the first boat out of Limasol." At that time, Max reckoned, there were enough young American warriors on the run in Europe to form a breakaway Peace Corps. A pair of deserters from the British Parachute Regiment would hardly have inflamed the Greek or the Turkish police.

"You never been on the run," Sergeant Todd said. "But I was. And they caught me, all right. That was the last time I got busted down to private."

"I didn't know."

"Lots of things you don't know, sir. If I'd kept my nose clean, I'd have been a sergeant major years ago."

Max looked at his watch. The plane was circling again, they were spending longer over the airport than they'd spent crossing the Alps. "You got nothing to worry about," Sergeant Todd said.

"You reckon?"

"Nothing. You're resigning your commission, right? You're jacking in the Army?"

"Too true," Max said. He had gone through the preliminaries before he left Arabia. If a small miracle happened, he would be a civilian within a matter of weeks. While other men burned autumn leaves, he would be pouring paraffin on all his Khaki garments and dropping a match on the lot.

"So you're all right," the sergeant said.

"Declare a public holiday." If it ever came out that Max had lied about the murder of the sergeant major, his resignation wouldn't help. "They could whip me back into the Army and court-martial me, one, one, two." His stomach told him that the plane was dropping. "But you know that, don't you, Sergeant? A latrine lawyer like you?"

"I was just trying to cheer you up, sir. I'd get a quicker laugh from a hearse."

They made an easy landing and disembarked in good order. It was unusual for Max Lawson's platoon to march like infantry. They saw themselves as hard men who'd left all the Army bull behind them. Still they moved with swank and swagger, showing off to the people behind the barrier. But Max's eye was on the officer who towered over the happy families. Major Hippisley was an airborne staff major, so big, so heavy and so sad that they called him Hippo.

"Max," Hippo said.

"You don't look too pleased to see me, Hippo."

"You won't be doing handstands when you hear my news," Major Hippisley said. "Put your sergeant in charge of your men." Todd overheard and carried on. "I've got to drive you somewhere." He led Max beyond a hangar and out of sight of the men.

"You're taking me to a knocking shop, I hope?"

"Already?" Major Hippisley asked. "I thought your heart was in Arabia?" He was referring to Max's affair, which had ended disastrously in Bahrain. For Hippisley this was an unusually snide remark. Max stared up at him, wondering how he'd heard about the woman.

"I'm taking you to meet a brigadier, I fear," Hippisley said. "From the Military Secretary's staff. The brigadier will arrange your posting."

"He'll arrange my posting *now?*" Max asked. "How about my disembarkation leave?"

"Later," Hippo said. "For an officer, leave is a privilege not a right, as you well know."

"But I've resigned from the Army, *sir.*"

"Not just yet you haven't. It takes time for that sort of thing to make its way through channels."

"Or sewers, sir?"

"I would laugh. Honestly, I would, I so enjoy your banter. Unfortunately I've got stitches in my mouth." Hippo had become Major Hippisley, the old friendly manner had gone.

"I don't feel like laughing, either, sir. I'm not feeling too well, you see. I'm going to report sick."

"On what grounds?"

"I'm unfit for airborne, sir," Max said. "Parachuting frightens me rigid. I'll have to tell the medical officer I can't go on."

Hippisley wearily dragged his beret to a more soldierly angle. "That's the lousiest excuse I've heard in a long time," he said. "And you haven't a hope in hell. Your record as an officer is third rate. As a parachutist you're first class and everybody knows it."

"I've changed, sir. I won't draw another parachute, I can't face it."

"And I wouldn't try to face the medical officer with a yarn like that if I were you."

"Sorry, sir. My nerve's gone. I'm unfit for airborne."

"I don't remember you saluting me, Lieutenant Lawson. That's better. Stand at ease, stand easy. I didn't hear that sick-report rhubarb. And don't repeat it."

"With all due respect, sir, I'm reporting sick."

"Keep your voice down," Major Hippisley said. "Look, I'm willing to overlook the fact that you've just disembarked from a military aircraft, dressed like a rat catcher. I haven't noticed that your hair's so long you make Che Guevara look like he was covering up his bald spot."

Max grinned.

"I'm not being funny," Hippisley said. "That's all I'll overlook. You're still a subaltern and you'll still obey orders.

"Yes, sir, very good, sir," Max said. "After I've reported sick, sir."

Major Hippisley led him through customs and into the deserted Army transport office, where he sat down at a desk which was too small for him. "You're determined to be court-martialled?" he asked. "Don't be in such a hurry, all that can be arranged in good time. Nobody's going to pretend that you covered yourself in glory out there in the Sands. But I'm doing my humble best for you." He pushed the desk away from his knees. "You were too young. You should never have been sent into a civil war in Akdhar...."

"Quite agree, sir. That's where my nerve went."

"Will you kindly listen to me? The one thing that didn't desert you in Arabia was your nerve. Let's not play silly bugger any longer. I've got all the reports. If you hadn't been such a damned fool at the end, you might have been in line for an MC."

Max was silent. In the Walter Mitty corner of his mind, he saw himself calling at the palace and telling the sovereign what to do with her Military Cross.

"I'm all for you leaving the Army quietly. And there's only one way you can do that. By obeying orders. You can query those orders later, once you've carried them out. You follow?"

"No, sir."

"You'll do as you're told. Otherwise I'll be dashing off a note of sympathy to your next of kin."

"Haven't got any kin, sir."

"No. Your father was in the Army and he had a rotten deal. Then you changed your name before you joined up." Max's surprise was too obvious. "You didn't expect to get away with that forever, did you? There are such things as genuine birth cerificates, you know. Tell me, were you intending to pay the Army back for what it did to your father?"

"I haven't got a father, sir."

"You're an indifferent liar, Lawson, and your face gives you away. You're ashamed of disowning your father, aren't you? And you haven't told him you were on your way home? Don't worry. We haven't told him either."

"I haven't got a father. He's dead."

Major Hippisley reached into the pocket of his battle-dress trousers, extracted a typewritten sheet and handed it over.

"All the details are there," he said. "What happened to your father. Your time at art school. The lies you told the recruiting board. Read it. Save us both unnecessary embarrassment."

Max glanced at the paper, pretending to be bored. He saw enough to know that the Army had him strapped across a gun carriage. "Ready to move off?" Major Hippisley asked.

"Yes, sir. To the medical officer."

"Don't be such a bloody bore or I'll take you under escort. Have you any civilian clothing? Go and change."

As he passed the window, Max saw his men moving off in trucks toward the leave centre, followed by an escort of family cars. He hadn't even been allowed to see them on their way. He could always contact Todd but the rest of the home addresses were in the platoon book, which the sergeant had in his rucksack.

He changed quickly and rejoined Major Hippisley in the Army transport office.

"Oh, my God," the staff major said. "You call that civilian clothing?"

"All I've got, sir."

90

"I must warn you that the brigadier isn't colour blind. Luckily for you, he's not bull-conscious, either."

"You still haven't named him, sir."

"Haven't I? How remiss of me. Brigadier Richard Murray-Strachan."

10

"KING'S ROAD," the staff major said. It was the first time he had begun the conversation since they left the airport and he hardly needed to tell Max they had entered the most over-rated thoroughfare in Southwest London.

"Thanks, I'm not sure I'd have recognised it." As he looked round, he wished *Time* magazine had never invented swinging London in general or kinky King's Road in particular. Now the rents were so high that almost all the small tradesmen's shops had gone and the King's Road looked like an elongated clothes store, with antique shops and restaurants for light relief. He wondered if the boutiques were all surface eruptions of one subterranean clothes factory. The restaurants looked too closely packed to the antique shops. Did late-night diners ever suffer from woodworm in the bisque?

"The whole of London's changed," Hippisley said. He had taken so long to answer that Max had forgotten his own remark. Looking at the girls, he realised he'd missed the last of the miniskirts and the whole of the hot-pants epoch.

Hippisley rounded Sloane Square slowly, ignoring the through traffic as if he were driving a tank. Then he turned left and stopped by a house in a back street between Knights-bridge and Chelsea. "We're not going in *here*?" Max asked.

"You are. I can't. I'm in uniform. Best of luck."

"You've got the wrong house," Max said. "Unless I'm see-ing things, this is the Special Air Service club. I don't like the members or the food. Even the building—that Knightsbridge Dutch effect?

"Go and ring the bell," Hippisley said.

"What's the password?" Max asked.

"Your humour's too sophisticated for me," Hippisley said. "I like broad comedy. I laugh like a horse when insolent young pricks get a jolly swift kick up the arse. Now *shift*."

As Max crossed the hall, he saw an obviously senior officer hanging up his bowler and his umbrella. "Max Lawson?" the senior officer asked. "Refreshingly punctual. Do come into the snug. My name is Murray-Strachan, by the way."

Max followed the brigadier into a small room with hearty armchairs in light and mellow leather. He noted that the walls were lined with cork, which ensured quiet and made bugging difficult. While he looked round, the brigadier put down his briefcase and pointed to an armchair. "I expect you drink whiskey?"

"Not often," Max said. "Thanks all the same, sir."

"This is a club. No 'sirs' and no rank, if you please. I'm afraid there's only whisky for the moment."

The brigadier struggled with the refined soda syphon. "Excuse me, won't you?" he asked. "I'm not exactly at home here, myself. The Special Air Service treat me as an honorary member when I happened to be held up in town. It's central, quite convenient, don't you agree?"

"Convenient for what?" Max asked but Murray-Strachan did not seem to hear. As he raised his glass, Max left his. "I'll have a glass of soda water, if I may." He helped himself.

"First of all, my heartiest congratulations," Murray-Strachan said.

"On what, sir . . . Mister Murray-Strachan?"

"Didn't Hippo tell you? Your application's been approved. You've been accepted by the Special Air Service."

"Sorry, but there's been some mistake. I never volunteered for the SAS."

"Your memory's at fault," Murray-Strachan said.

"It's not and I've resigned my commission."

The brigadier sighed, then he raised his trousers a little so that the creases would not be sullied by his knees. "Your resignation has not yet been accepted, your papers are still on the factory floor."

"Haven't they been minced by the machinery?"

"Aren't you pushing your luck, Lawson?"

"I can't see how. I've none to push." Max knew that the SAS always had far more volunteers than they could absorb. He was also fairly certain that he was one of the few Parachute Regiment subalterns who had never even dreamed of joining them.

"The records show that you volunteered." The brigadier's eyes were cold and blue but his lips suggested he was mildly amused.

"Then the records have been forged," Max said.

"I didn't catch that, Lawson."

"I said that the records have been forged, Mister Murray-Strachan."

"Sorry but I didn't hear you. I lost my ear trumpet at Omdurman. Or was it the siege of Ladysmith? I can't recall. Don't bother to repeat your remark."

"I won't. But there's something I can do," he said. "Slap in a Section 41 Complaint. To the Sovereign against illegal orders."

Murray-Strachan nodded. "No need to instruct me in the Army Act," he said. "I suppose you appreciate that a complaint to the Queen must pass through your own battalion commander? Then it proceeds through your brigade commander and on and up through channels? On the way that complaint might gather dust on my desk."

"I'm in no hurry to join the SAS. Use my 41 Complaint for a bookmark if you like."

"I don't need reminders, as I said. And you've already threatened a senior officer with a Section 41 complaint." Max was startled. He'd made that threat in Arabia and the commanding officer concerned was now dead.

"You may well find that a Section 41 Complaint can misfire, blow up in your face, so to speak. In point of fact, it usually does. Don't you know that your brigade commander would personally bite your head off? Then he'd have the head salted and stuck up on a pike at Aldershot if the War Office allowed him?" Murray-Strachan no longer seemed amused. "You don't want to face two court-martials, I shouldn't think?"

"One or two, what's the difference?" Max asked.

Murray-Strachan studied the subaltern's face. If one ignored the hairstyle and the outlandish clothing, Lawson looked more mature than his years or his Army record suggested. In the brigadier's view, Lawson's eyes were distinctly mad. He was a mass of nervous energy, he never sat still and his brow was beginning to crease heavily at the age of twenty-one. It was time to apply pressure, much as the brigadier deplored the whole affair.

"I take your point," Murray-Strachan said. "The second court-martial offence would be trivial compared with the first. We have all the details of the murder of Sergeant Major O'Donnell."

"I wish I had," Max said.

"Oh, we know you weren't close enough to kill him or even to see who did it," Murray-Strachan said. "We also know that we'd have quite a job to prove the murderer's guilt. Not that it matters."

"No?" Max was so surprised that he allowed the brigadier to put whiskey into his soda.

"It's not unknown for a sergeant major to be shot in the back by a bolshie soldier," Murray-Strachan said. "We're more interested in the collusion and the conspiracy which followed. It's very rare for an officer and his sergeant to attempt to suppress the evidence. Don't you agree?"

Max concentrated on his drink.

"We have an alternative. We can court-martial you, your sergeant and your entire platoon . . . *some* of them must be innocent, simply too scared to tell the truth. Seems a pity to send them all to jail. Perhaps not for so many years as you or Todd will serve inside but long enough for innocent men. You follow?"

"Closely," Max said. "If I join the Special Air Service, what happens about the charges?"

"All dropped," Murray-Strachan said. "The whole affair can be forgotten if you'll simply do an easy job. Not beyond the capacity of a Boy Scout."

"Then why not use a Boy Scout?" Max asked. His hatred of the SAS was rising. He had never cared for that regiment or for its political role or for its espionage activities. He had never fancied their habit of dropping into foreign and un-friendly territory from as high as eight miles up by free fall to cheat the local radar installations. On the screens, a body dropping at that speed looked no more significant than a dead bird. Max had no desire to join the SAS on their dizzy drops or at the rendezvous they made with their comrades *before* their parachutes opened as low as 2,500 feet. Nor could he accept their principle that a wounded comrade on a free-fall spying foray should be killed immediately since the others could neither leave him behind to be captured nor carry him with them. . . .

"Are you with me again?" Murray-Strachan asked. "Did you know your lips move when you're talking to yourself?"

"Sorry but I can't find anybody else who speaks my language," Max said. "I don't believe you'll court-martial the whole platoon. I think you know who killed the sergeant major. If you don't, nobody does. You'll do the murderer and me and Sergeant Todd. Fair enough. Court-martialling the rest would be bad for morale and worse for the regiment's image."

"I may have to take that chance, Lawson."

"I don't think you will. And if you do, you'll find the Parachute Regiment in arms. They'll make sure the men are pretty bloody well defended."

"Are you suggesting insubordination from your entire regiment?"

"My regiment doesn't believe in having shit thrown at them, sir. One of the battalions mutinied twice for good reasons. And the whole of an airborne division almost mutinied in Palestine."

"*Almost* mutinied? For a good reason?" Murray-Strachan asked. "They meant to blow a Jewish village apart, if my memory serves me. I was there, as it happens and we surrounded the entire division with artillery and tanks. The Israelis must have thought it very strange." His smile was strengthening again. "How odd," he said. "A defence of the regiment from you. I imagine there's a jingoist hidden somewhere beneath that fancy shirt."

"I doubt that. And I'm not joining the SAS. I'm scared of parachuting."

He thought that Hippisley had half-believed that story, but Murray-Strachan simply laughed and the cork walls deadened the sound. "I know your record, Lawson. You've had two dangerous parachuting reports."

"That's how fear took me," Max said.

"I'm inclined to doubt that," the brigadier said. "I rather imagine you'd be one of those who die laughing."

Max winced at the allusion, a joke in bad taste that no fellow parachutist would ever make. Murray-Strachan was a penguin, a crap-hat who hadn't parachuted and therefore was unworthy of respect. As soon as he formed the thought, Max realised he was reasoning like a Mafioso. But free-falling parachutists who left the plane at eight thousand feet used oxygen breathing gear. Some men had found such pleasure in breathing pure oxygen that they'd forgotten to open their parachutes in time and had been splattered all over the dropping zone. They had probably died laughing.

"Rest assured, no parachuting will be involved," the brigadier said.

"Oh, Christ," Max said. According to some, another Special Air Service function was to kill where and when they were told. Some newspaper had been tipped off, tried to print the reports and had its fingers severely burned. The SAS were also thought to be directly involved with the most powerful men in Whitehall. In theory they were always responsible to the local area commander. But he'd heard that they sometimes answered directly to Downing Street or to military intelligence. As Max saw it, they were responsible to everyone and therefore to no one. He feared their growing power, particularly since the Official Secrets Act had been invoked to keep most Special Air Service operations under wraps. . . .

"You mentioned Christ?" Murray-Strachan asked. "In what connection?"

"This one, *sir*. I'm killing no one, anywhere, at any time for you or anybody else. You can court-martial the whole of the Army. You can screw my balls off. Or you can boil them with me still attached. But I'm killing nobody and that's that."

Murray-Strachan lit a pipe, his first of the day. He drew on it until the smoke was drifting blue, then he looked at Max with what might have passed for sympathy. Privately he was sorry for the boy and privately he could not remember another subaltern who could use the word "sir" with such offence.

"I fear you've been misinformed," the brigadier said. "I've heard the rumours, we all have. But there are no SAS execution squads. That was the figment of someone's tortured imaginings."

"I'm killing no one."

"You killed in Arabia," Murray-Strachan said.

"In action and by mistake and I won't make that mistake again."

Murray-Strachan crossed the room to press the bell. The brigadier walked swiftly, he had been trained in light infantry with a marching style of 160 paces to the minute.

"Forget about killing," Murray-Strachan said. "Your job is to help preserve life, not to take it. Have you forgotten that the SAS also guard members of the Royal Household, senior statesmen and important visitors to this country?"

"No, I haven't." The SAS often acted as secret guardians for very important persons. They did not always reveal their presence to the Special Branch of the police or to normal counterterrorist elements or even to the very important persons they were guarding. . . .

The waiter answered Murray-Strachan's summons. "My guest doesn't care for whisky," the brigadier said. "Perhaps you'd like to order, Mister Lawson."

"A Coca-Cola," Max said, "with lots of ice, a slice of lemon and two straws." The waiter hurriedly withdrew.

"You see?" Max said, "I don't know how to behave like an officer and gentleman. What kind of guardian would I make?"

Murray-Strachan sat down and pulled his armchair so close that Max caught a whiff of after-shave lotion. Typical of this bastard brigadier to shave twice a day. "Exactly the guardian I want," he said. "It so happens that you—unlike your clothes —are custom-built for the job. The first essential is that the guardian should not look like an Army officer and I think you'll agree that you don't."

"Good of you to say so, *sir*. I wouldn't even pass as a guard at the civil airports."

"What are you talking about?" Murray-Strachan asked.

"I think you know, sir." Since the hijacking of airliners had become a growth industry, he'd heard that the SAS had taken over security at some civil airports, another breach of British custom. "And I've got the wrong accent for Dublin."

"I've lost you again," the brigadier said but his expression made it clear that he hadn't. The rumour was that some of the atrocities committed in Dublin and blamed on the Irish Republican Army had been carried out by the SAS to shift Southern Irish sympathy swiftly and violently from the IRA. But there was no proof of this. Rumors about the SAS were always rife throughout the Army. The regiment was feared,

respected but never liked, and the Army had borrowed gangster slang to name them. They were known as the Frighteners. . . .

"Shall we try concentrating?" the brigadier asked. He
opened his briefcase with a key on a chain from his pocket
while Max wondered what kind of mooring the chain had. It
was probably sunk into cement.

"Now, the American visitor to be guarded was in the British Army in wartime and he can smell a pair of Army boots at
twenty paces. You take the point? We want him looked after
but we don't want him to know. He thinks he's quite capable
of looking after himself and he may kick up a fuss."

"Don't tell me any more," Max said, "I'm not buying and I
don't want to know." The brigadier ignored him and produced some papers from his case.

"Read them at your leisure," he said. Murray-Strachan
crossed to the side table and looked up the cricket news while
Max studied the court-martial indictments. All of his platoon
were in it to their eyeballs and the dice were loaded. The
suggested defending officers were the most obsequious dead-
beats Aldershot could muster. There was also a letter, sealed
and addressed to Max's father, giving his proper surname and
his present address.

"Read enough?" Murray-Strachan asked. "I'd rather not
waste any more time." He produced a range of colour photographs of a man in his late forties or early fifties with red hair
and a memorable face. There was something more than wild-
ness in those features. As Max studied the photographs taken
from different angles, he also saw that the face was asymetri-
cal. It was as if there was a central fault in the skull so that
one side of the face had slipped a fraction, producing two
unlike profiles and a full face slightly off true.

Max turned the photographs over and read an innocent,

potted version of Middlemass's life which made him sound quite interesting. He noted that Middlemass was five feet nine inches with a 48-inch chest.

"What do you see?" Murray-Strachan asked.

"Somebody I wouldn't want to meet in the dark."

"Well, he's a bit of a rough diamond, perhaps."

"And he owns a few well-polished ones as well."

"The note makes it clear that he's an investment banker," the brigadier said. "Rich and perfectly respectable."

"So you want me to go to Wall Street and guard his office door?"

"Middlemass is in this country," the brigadier said. "Living at Rookwood, in the south. You don't know the area, do you?"

"No." For once he was able to be unhelpful while telling the truth.

"But you're interested in wildlife?"

"Night life, you mean?"

"I don't propose to lose my temper. Don't waste your time. You know about birds, fallow deer, foxes and so on."

"Not much."

"You're a good amateur and so is Middlemass."

"Wouldn't he find more to see at home?"

"He might, but he happens to be in England on business. He's an anti-blood-sport man. A rather amusing idea. Aren't you?"

"Yes," Max said.

"Odd enthusiasm for an Army officer, isn't it?"

"Thanks again," Max said. Not only was he in a trap but the bait was stinking. Why would they go to this trouble to place him in such a job?

"And you're rather keen on Hardy?"

Max was impressed, despite himself. The brigadier had

done his homework on a lowly subaltern. "Laurel and Hardy?" he asked.

"I've told you I shall not lose my temper, Lawson. On the other hand, I could make life harder for you than you can possibly imagine. I'm talking about Thomas Hardy. Wessex and all that, the Rookwood area. You've read almost everything Hardy wrote."

"May I ask how you know that?"

"You may not. But you're just the sort of chap to strike up an acquaintance with Middlemass."

"Why?" Max asked.

"An intelligent question at last," Murray-Strachan said. "Middlemass is arranging an important oil deal with our chaps in the City of London."

"And he needs a guard against bowlers and umbrellas? Or against English business methods?" Max reckoned that the brigadier would not waste time by punishing him . . . not yet. ·

"You know there is a permanent battle going on for the oil fields in the Middle East?"

"I know a little, sir . . . I've just been involved in one of the scruffier sideshows. In Akdhar. You have their oil now. Congratulations."

"Every country's fighting to get their hands on the oil. *Our* hands are tolerably clean as you know."

"I was in no position to judge."

"Nor are you now. Simply take my word for it that forty percent of all the oil the Americans use will come from the Middle East within the next ten years. And we have an understanding with the Americans."

"The natural relationship. Of course."

"But we don't have a natural relationship with Arab terrorists, Lawson. They want to dominate their oil fields."

"I wonder why?" Max asked.

"If they can kill Robert Kennedy and wreck the Olympic Games, they call kill Middlemass at Rookwood, unless he's properly guarded."

Max did not bother to answer. How was he supposed to guard a man like Middlemass against exploding envelopes and poisoned letters? Or nasty little mines like Gravel, which were about the size of a tea bag and blended with the earth until someone trod on one and lost his foot?

How was he supposed to disarm the booby traps, which could be inside any rusty old can? Or the more artistic bombs which looked like dried cow dung and went off at the tremor of someone dodging them to keep his shoes clean?

"Other people will look after the main elements of security." The brigadier appeared to be reading his mind. "Your job will simply be to get to know Middlemass and stay with him as closely as possible on his night walks and his dawn walks or whatever enthusiastic naturalists do. Your only responsibility will be to watch for suspicious characters and report to your controlling officer."

"Who is?"

"You'll know in good time." The brigadier had noted that Max hadn't asked a single question about Arab terrorists. He would need to be as closely watched as Middlemass himself.

Murray-Strachan rose. "Your controlling officer will contact you tomorrow morning," he said. "A room has been booked for you for tonight, quite near here. You can walk to the Royal Court Hotel, I trust?"

"I think so." Max had never known a subaltern to be lodged in a good London hotel at the Army's expense.

"This will be your last night in London for some time. Enjoy yourself, but don't overdo it."

Max nodded and made for the door.

"One last thing," Murray-Strachan said. "Do as you are told and you will be out of the Army in no time. You can't wait for that and neither can I."

The waiter knocked and entered diffidently. "Your drink, sir," he said to Max. The Coca Cola was in a tankard and the straws were artistically arranged.

11

LAURENCE ADAM WORKED the leather bellows briskly but the elm logs in the library fire did not respond.

"Are you still toying with that glass, Shona?" he asked.

"It keeps my hands active, I don't knit," she said. They had been booting the conversation along ever since Adam returned to his house and found that not only Middlemass but his daughter had arrived. It was clear that Shona's clothing upset the squire of Rookwood, he was not used to having a lady in his library in jeans, a man's shirt and a Mexican blanket poncho. Shona felt sorry for him, but how could she tell him that she had dropped her father at the airport, parked the Chevvy and caught the first commercial flight that would take her?

"Warm enough?" Adam asked, after a pause.

"Toasting," she said and he almost caught her eye then let his glance slide again. Her father was silent, looking upward, apparently mesmerised by the bad baroque of the library ceiling. She knew that he was working something out, but Adam was unused to people who could lose themselves in company as completely as his guest and he had tried Shona on every subject from women's liberation to the energy crisis while he glanced over her head or round her ear. She knew what was coming next. Modern art. Adam knew that she painted and Shona was bracing herself for the ordeal when the telephone rang.

"Rookwood House," Adam said. "I'll just find out." Without covering the mouthpiece adequately, he said to Middlemass "Are you here? Some *woman*."

Middlemass reluctantly accepted the phone. "Yes?" he asked.

"It's Mrs. Walters, sir." Middlemass considered hanging up then he realised that would suggest panic to the men who were monitoring his calls.

"Mrs. Walters? Oh, yes. Aren't you Harry Walters' wife? Didn't we meet once?" he asked. "How is he? Sorry I didn't have time to call in at the office."

"He told me never to telephone to you but I have to speak to you now," she said.

"I can't think why he said that, Mrs. Walters," Middlemass said. "I've got a close relationship with my London staff. I like to keep in touch with them *and* their families." He was surprised that Walters had given his wife the number.

"He would have rung me by now," Mrs. Walters said. "He promised."

"You mean he's not home? Don't worry, Mrs. Walters. I expect he's . . ." The line went dead but Middlemass talked on. ". . . Working late at the office. No trouble, I do assure you. Phone me any time." Middlemass wished the dead telephone good-night and hung up.

"Have you seen Laurence's paintings, Shona?" he asked. "He has a pretty wide range. English painters of the eighteenth and early nineteenth century. Not exactly the Mellon collection but it's impressive."

Shona glared at him, with her back to Adam. "I didn't know you collected, Mr. Adam," she said.

"I have a few paintings," he said. "Would you care to see them?"

"Very much," Shona said. Her back was still turned to Adam and she bared her teeth at her father.

"You coming, John?" Adam asked.

"No, I think I'll take a walk," Middlemass said. He left the house in search of another phone, walking on the grass instead of the gravel drive so that he would not alert the dogs at the lodge house where the gamekeeper lived. Middlemass walked down the road for half a mile and stopped by the old schoolhouse. Rookwood School had been closed for many years and the house was now occupied by a retired grocer and his wife. Middlemass tapped on the door.

"I'm sorry to bother you," he said to the grocer.

"No trouble. Mister Middlemass, isn't it? Good to see you back." They had drunk together in the Rookwood Arms on Middlemass's last visit. "Come on in."

"It's the phone at the house," Middlemass said, "It's not working very well."

"Don't expect me to faint," the grocer said. "Every time a wind blows some bloody beech branch falls across the line. Help yourself." He pointed to the telephone. "We'll have a jar when you're ready."

First Middlemass tried dialling 352 then the telephone number in front of him. This time there were no distinct clicks. Then he tried the number where Walters should have been. He dialled the emergency alternatives but Walters was not to be found. Middlemass phoned over a "birthday greetings cable," to his man in Zurich. This was the warning to stay away.

12

MAX KICKED A MATCHBOX along the bedroom carpet. He had
to think this out and he had no intention of propping the
hotel bar, watched by some SAS shit in a sombre suit. He
couldn't even be certain of identifying the man. He had met
a few of them in his time and none of them looked like free-
falling desperadoes. A fair number of them were jump
happy, they had to go on and on parachuting as other men
needed to drink, but it didn't usually show in their appearance or even in casual conversation. On the whole, SAS men
were well mannered and well dressed. They didn't drink
heavily and they didn't brawl, for if they were ever provoked
into fighting in public, they were screwed by their senior
officers. Although Max had met a few killers in his time and
seen their deeds written in their faces, this did not apply to
the SAS men he'd met. They were inclined to be fresh-faced
lads and their officers talked and acted like self-assured young
nothings in the city.

But Max knew Chelsea, he had been at art school there,
and SAS men would be spotted in his favorite pub like any
other stranger. When he left the hotel he made directly for
his old local, which never changed. The brewers who owned
it had tried that but had been dissuaded by the customers

111

shunning the place. In the public bar Max ordered himself a large scotch and a pint of draught lager to drown it, then sat in the quiet corner commanding the door. He hadn't bought a word of Murray-Strachan's story. He couldn't think why the brigadier should want him within a thousand miles of an important American visitor. But this line of speculation led nowhere so he considered the court martial indictment the brigadier had shown him. Unless the Army had gone mad, there were two possibilities. One was that the courts-martial would be held and that no brigadier had any power to stop them. The second . . . the more likely premise . . . was that the indictments were phoney, an elaborate forgery on borrowed Army forms. If they were phoney . . . Max hoped that the pub's most boring drunk hadn't seen him as he stopped in front of an inoffensive drinker of indeterminate sex.

"Are you a man or a woman?" the drunk asked.

"What does it matter so long as I know?" the person asked and walked out of the bar. Max decided that leaning on the drunk would be a waste of energy. Instead he ordered another pint of lager and a sausage, remembering he hadn't eaten since Cyprus, remembering too late that he had no head for drink on an empty stomach. He was losing the thread of the court-martial argument and thinking about Middlemass again. So far as he knew, political assassination in Britain was very rare, other than the work carried out quietly by the state, but the situation was deteriorating fast. The very presence of the SAS was a reminder that Britain was drifting with the rest of the world toward official and unofficial violence. Some police forces were even being armed with shotguns and the old truce on firearms between the police and the criminals was going with the rest. Britain was no longer quiet and dull, drizzly and mild. It was becoming coldly, chillingly violent. But there was still very little chance of a well-guarded visitor being knocked off in the southern back-woods. . . .

The pub bore was by the bar and he had reached the stage of telling limericks. His voice rose as he declaimed:

> *There was a young fellow from Ryde,*
> *Who fell down a crapper and died.*

The landlord appeared and nodded to two Irish barmen. The boring drunk ended outside within seconds, but the incident had derailed Max's train of thought. He ordered himself another large whisky and another pint of lager, just as a hand fell on his shoulder.

"Max Lawson," the Irish publican said. "As scruffy as ever. And I heard you were in the Army nowadays?"

"You did?"

"That's the wicked story they've been telling about you," the publican said, "and if you're a brown job, you're barred. You know my rules, Max. No proofs, no soldiers, no IRA men in here."

"I'm not in the Army any longer," Max said. "Listen, Fergus, you sure there aren't any redcaps in this bar?"

"In here? There will be leprechauns dancing on the tip of my tool before you'll see military policemen here, you drunken sot."

"No SAS?"

Fergus stared at him. "Frighteners? In here? They'd wait a month before they caught my barman's eye. Are you trying to insult me? Are you asking to be barred?"

"I'm on the trot," Max suddenly said, for the drink was getting to him even faster than he'd feared.

"You've deserted, you crazy cunt? But officers can't desert, now, can they?"

"This one has." When Fergus turned up, he had been uncertain how to act. Now he knew that he couldn't help the men of his platoon whatever he did. Now he knew he was going to run.

"Keep your voice down," the publican said.

"I'm whispering," Max said.

"Is that what you call it? They'll hear you at the War Office if you whisper any louder. Get upstairs and ask Nancy to give you a coffee. A straight coffee. Not an Irish coffee. And don't venture down again till Nance gives you the word. We often get the peelers in at this hour of the night. Drinks on the house while they're getting ready to book you, the bastards."

"You telling me that the Chelsea police would talk to Redcaps, Fergus?"

"Things have changed, Max. Things are getting worse and worse. The police are being civil to the military police and I've even heard that the Inland Revenue are on speaking terms with the Exchange Control. The country's going to the dogs. Upstairs. I was in the Army once, myself."

"So was I," Max said. He made his way uncertainly up the narrow staircase but the publican's wife was not in their living quarters so he forced himself to make and drink a cup of coffee. He was reaching the crafty stage of drunkenness and he reasoned it would be stupid to attempt to bolt that night. He would go back to the Royal Court Hotel, sleep it off then go down to Rookwood with his escort in the morning. In the woods there he would wait for his chance then skip to the southwest, making for Cornwall. He wouldn't try to cross to France immediately. He would hang around in the southwest for a week or two in the biggest Cornish camping site he could find. The camp near Penzance was the one, large enough to have its own dance hall and acres of semiperma-

114

nent caravans with wrought, taut gates and economy-size lawns. No one would look for him there before the time came to slip away for France from one of the smaller Cornish private ports. Padstow maybe. . . .

As the second cup of coffee burned his lips, he worried about Todd and he couldn't find the publican's private telephone. Max emptied his pockets on Fergus's table, sorted out his coins and waltzed towards the phone booth on the stairway.

By closing one eye he was able to read the new code for Aldershot and he dialled with care and craft. He was surprised to get the right number at his first attempt and even more surprised to hear the voice of Margaret Todd who was supposed to have run off with another man.

"Yes?" Mrs. Todd's voice was unmistakable. "If you're phoning about the payments on the washing machine . . ."

"I'm not. This is Max. Max Lawson."

She did not answer but he could hear her laboured breathing and he got a second coin handy in case she stayed too long on the canvas and counted out the call.

"Mr. Lawson? My husband's platoon commander?"

"That was the theory."

"You don't sound like yourself, Mr. Lawson."

"I don't feel like myself either. Does your husband happen to be around?"

"Where else would he be?" Margaret Todd's voice was hectoring and shrill, she had always been a born diplomat, the perfect wife for garrison life, a launching pad for her husband's career.

"Nowhere else," Max said. "I was joking. Can I talk to him, please?"

"He's busy and you've been drinking," she said. Max heard a scuffle then Todd came on the line.

"That you, sir?"

"Yes. And the balloon's gone up. The ball's on the slates."

"I know," Todd said. "I've been wondering how to get in touch."

"You, too?"

"Scarface. He's been sniffing round." Todd was talking about the military police officer who had first investigated the sergeant major's death.

"Sure it was him?"

"I'm sure. I was on my way back from the boozer when I saw him and I've got this funny idea that he wanted me to see him and he hoped I would panic."

"So you've got the message? They're after us."

"Seems so." Todd said.

"I'm going to take a little stroll," Max said. "Maybe we'll meet up in Katmandu."

"Nothing doing," Todd said. "That's what they want us to do. Get a flap up and run for it. Then they'll nail us. Right?"

"I'm taking a chance on my boots holding out," Max said. "I've been ordered to a place called Rookwood. In the woods. A fair old springboard."

"That's it. One deep dive and you'll crack your nut off the bottom."

The time pips sounded and the line went dead. Max was redialling the number when someone rapped on the kiosk glass. He lost count of the telephone digits as the rapping became more insistent and an Irish barman beckoned him from the kiosk door. "Fergus wants you," he said. "Upstairs. Can you make it? Will you be alright now?"

Fergus was at his table, stuffing the contents of Max's pockets into a bag. He had even left his passport on the table. "That's yours," the publican said, "look after it. Nip into the saloon bar, quiet as you can and talk to the girl in the black plastic mac."

"I'm not a plastic coat man, Fergus. My taste in sex is simpler."

"You'll be tasting no sex of any kind at all if you're not more bloody careful. Do as I tell you or you're barred. Barred from this pub for life. You understand?"

"For Christ's sake, Fergus. That's sadistic."

"Shift. The saloon bar or the door," Fergus said.

The girl in the black plastic mac was recognisably a member of the God Squad. She had long brown hair and she'd been working on the pre-Raphaelite expression. Max noted that and then, a moment later, he decided she was beautiful.

"I'm Ellen," she said. "You want to leave the Army?" She was talking intensely but so quietly that Max was forced to lipread in the noisy bar. "You want an end to violence?"

"No," Max said. "I've one or two blokes to mince before I settle down. But I don't hold with organised violence. Official, legal violence, that's disgusting."

"I can see you're very disturbed," Ellen said. "I'm going to take you home with me and . . ."

"Don't tell me any more," Max said. "Surprise me."

"Don't be silly. I'm going to take you home and tell you all about the organisation."

"You've got it wrong. That's what I'm leaving."

"Not that kind of organisation," Ellen said. "We're underground."

Max looked at the smoky ceiling and the dim lights. "I knew it wasn't my eyesight," he said.

"Oh, come along." Ellen had an open sports car and the fresh air seemed to help him. At first the streetlights were blurred then he saw them clearly and then they developed a

117

cinematic impact as Ellen turned down a quiet street between the King's Road and the river.

In the past the cottages in this quiet street had been dwellings for workmen but the area had risen in prestige and the cottages were occupied by ambitious men and embalmed in many coats of paint. Ellen stopped outside the only house that was not painted. Instead it had honeysuckle, passion flower and Russian vine climbing up the trellis from the basement to the roof.

"Who grew the jungle?" Max asked.

"I did. You mind?"

"No, I like it, I think it's very practical for . . ." He wanted to say that honeysuckle blossom would kill the smell of cats' piss and dog shit in this area so heavily patrolled by animal owners and their pets but he didn't want to offend her.

"Come in and be quiet," Ellen led the way to the kitchen, then made him coffee and scrambled eggs while she explained how her group helped deserters. The men on the run were Americans on the whole, but Ellen reckoned there was nothing in the rules against helping a compatriot. Max was growing interested when the street door began to shake.

"Oh, my goodness," Ellen said. "Friends of my brother. I do wish they wouldn't barge in here at any time of night."

Max followed casually as she opened the door, then two young men burst in. He felt that he had seen the first one somewhere before, possibly in the foyer of the Royal Court Hotel. The second man he knew too well. Major Robin Wainright usually looked at other men without seeing them, he seemed to be studying his reflection in an invisible mirror about three inches from his nose. For all that, he was the most dedicated of the Special Air Service free-fall parachutists, so noted for his obsession that he was known as the Sky Eater at Abingdon and beyond.

"Hullo, Max," Major Wainright said. He was ignoring Ellen; women embarrassed him easily. "Come on home, it's past your bedtime."

As Ellen clung to Max, the second SAS officer removed her arm, gently and courteously in the fashion of his regiment. "Max has to be up early," he said. "He talks awful rot when he's drunk but he's a frightfully good officer. Sorry he can't stay."

In the narrow street, the SAS officers sauntered on either side of Max, suggesting three men on a stroll between pubs. At the corner, a young giant in a ragged fur coat was twisting the radio aerial of a vintage Alvis coupé.

"I'd rather you didn't do that," Wainright said, casually.

"What's it to you, you upper class fart?"

"I don't care for vandalism," Wainright said, "or for fancy dress phonies from the slums parading up and down Chelsea, annoying the residents. You follow me? Move."

The man stared down at Wainright. "Piss off or I'll blow on you." He moved back in a karate defensive shuffle, which looked good to Max, but the Sky Eater simply laughed until the man forgot his karate position and aimed a kick. As Wainright grabbed his foot, the man hit the pavement with his skull.

"You still there?" Wainright asked him. "Good." He leaned over the man, unzipped his fly and pulled his penis. As Max moved from the shadows to intervene, the second SAS officer placed a pistol muzzle at the back of Max's neck. It was another casual gesture, but Max understood.

"Can you still hear me?" Wainright asked. "Try to answer, there's a good chap. Thank you. Just remember this in future. Don't try brawling with strangers, it's frightfully unwise."

They continued their leisurely stroll towards their car, an

anonymous Mini. While his colleague drove, the Sky Eater sat in the back with Max.

"You rotten bastard," Max said. "You could have killed him."

"But I didn't. One thing I don't care for is unnecessary violence."

"Why did you bother?"

"Because someone who holds the Queen's Commission behaves as a good citizen when he wears civilian clothes."

"An SAS man isn't allowed to fight civilians. Not for pleasure."

"No witnesses. Don't be such a bloody bore."

"I was a witness."

"You don't count. And by the way, this desertion talk of yours . . ."

Max's anger guttered and went out. "That was patter. I was trying to make the girl, that's all."

"I know that," the Sky Eater said. "But I wouldn't advise you to try that line again. Quite honestly, I wouldn't."

13

MIDDLEMASS MADE HIMSELF CONSPICUOUS on the high terrace of Rookwood House, looking out on the beech, the oaks and the yew as though he were savouring the morning. He still hadn't caught up on his sleep, he was aware that the trap was closing on him, but he had to look relaxed for his invisible audience.

Through the night and the early morning, he'd sat by his radio set, waiting for Zurich to acknowledge his warning. At six, he had stripped the set and found it had been expertly sabotaged, so that it *appeared* to be in working order. Obviously it had been taken from his locked trunk, either at Rookwood or in transit. Sleet, or someone, had known he was heading for Rookwood, artistically wrecked the set, tapped Adam's telephone, then jumped Walters. Rookwood, the sanctuary, had become an open prison. They would expect him to run and he'd no intention of obliging them just yet. They wouldn't risk killing him while his "dead man's vengeance" was still primed, but they could hold him. If he moved too fast, he would be running scared and they would trap him. The last advantage Rookwood had was that he couldn't be spirited away without the locals knowing.

Meanwhile, the air was bracing, with the first hint of winter on the wind and the birds were returning from the fields to the fat and nuts on the bird table. A nuthatch joined the tits, then a bullfinch. Even the jackdaws were skulking, mob-handed, just out of shotgun range. Although they lived in the elms by Rookwood House, the jackdaws never grew careless in the presence of men. The boldest of them began to close on the dangling fat, approaching with the usual sinister side-step, keeping watch like a tennis spectator. It had reason to be cautious. There were no longer any rooks in Rookwood, nor a single carrion crow. . . .

"Good morning, John." His host had joined him on the terrace. "You're the early worm that gets the bird, I see." Adam was pleased with his joke and Middlemass rewarded him with a smile. It was almost incredible that the opposition should recruit the bat-brained squire of Rookwood, but who else had known that Middlemass was on his way there? How otherwise could his set have been sabotaged and the tele-phone tapped before he had arrived and before Walters was snatched?

"Fancy a little rough shooting, today?" Laurence Adam asked.

"No thanks, I don't shoot."

"Nonsense, my dear fellow. There's this newish automatic sight. Use it and you just can't miss. It's as foolproof as one of those Japanese cameras."

"I don't shoot. On principle," Middlemass said. He found sincerity unavoidable at times.

"Don't think I don't understand," Adam said. "I simply can't stand people peppering fallow deer with ordinary shot."

"Good to hear that." Middlemass had read that the fallow deer in Rookwood were mentioned in the Domesday book. One theory was that the deer had been introduced locally by the Twelfth Roman Legion.

122

"Naturally the deer have to be kept down," Adam said. "They can be a frightful nuisance, you know. Rubbing their velvet on young trees and so on. They've wrecked my young red cedars already."

Adam was talking about his thuya trees, which had clearly been nibbled by a plague of starving rabbits, but Middlemass let it pass. "We have to cull the deer, keep their numbers within reason. Pity, but there it is," Adam said.

"Using a marksman with a stalker's rifle, I suppose?" Middlemass said. He had not intended to bait Adam but he had caught the flash of the binoculars from the wood and he was interested in snipers at that moment.

"Quite honestly, old chap, my funds don't run to marksmen. But my estate workers are jolly good and I always insist they use BB shot."

"That so?" Middlemass knew that the use of BB shot on deer was cruel. Wounded deer might linger for months with freshly grown hair covering their crippling wounds. "I think I'll take a walk."

"You aren't waiting for Shona?"

"I imagine she'll sleep until noon," Middlemass said. "She thinks nine A.M. is the middle of the night. I'm not going far, just taking in the view."

Adam grew expansive for it was his view, he owned it. "Must be a pleasant change after the States," he said.

"It is," Middlemass said, although he considered the fall in New England much more beautiful than the Rookwood autumn.

"Have a good look at the yews," Adam said. "Did you know that English longbows were made from the yews in my wood?"

"Imagine that." If Middlemass's sources were correct, English longbows had come from Spanish yews and the Rookwood yews had been originally planted to blanket the smell of privies and the putrefaction from shallow graves. Why the hell did he have to think about graves? His mood was darkening as the clouds hid the sun, he couldn't shake the feeling that he didn't have long to live. Although he believed Otsch Gellner that his tumour had been benign and although he did not expect to die violently at Sleet's hand, his instinct told him that death was at hand. His instinct had rarely betrayed him. Death was nothing, only the manner of dying was important. Somehow he had to win the Doha game, then leave them, laughing. . . .

"Enjoy your walk," Adam said. "Not going as far as the motorway, I don't suppose?"

"I don't think so."

"Pity, you're interested in hawks, aren't you?"

"Yes." Middlemass couldn't remember mentioning that to Adam.

"I gather there's a duck hawk on the motorway."

"A what?"

"A sparrow hawk," Adam said. "They've taken to the motorways to keep away from rifles, so I'm told. There's one rather wedded to our local stretch of road, I'm told."

Middlemass nodded and wandered off. In the first place a duck hawk was not a sparrow hawk. In the second, the main roads of England would be used by kestrels rather than sparrow hawks. How could Adam be so ignorant of his estate? He had even heard him complain about the wild clematis, which he called honeysuckle.

He made a detour to the south, cut back west in the cover of the hazel thickets, then he almost fell across a trip wire with an illegal gin trap close by it and a badger snare just beyond. Middlemass had been at the pub the night before, to persuade whoever it concerned that he was unhurried and unsuspicious. According to the public bar naturalists in the Rookwood Arms, the only badger earth in that belt had been poisoned. Besides, the snares were staggered instead of being placed for badgers along a run. The snares were also set too high for badgers, clearly intended to give stravaiging dogs a lingering death.

Death, there it was again. Why the hell did he bother to walk in the woods? Why didn't he just stroll around graveyards?

Middlemass heard the man before he saw him and he began a stalk, his steps muffled by the carpet of rotting beech mould. The stranger wore a green parka, he was armed with a pair of heavy wire cutters and he seemed totally engrossed. As Middlemass moved in on him, the man wrecked a badger snare beyond repair, raised his cutters in an obscene gesture then stood back to admire his work.

"Having fun?" Middlemass asked.

"Yes," the stranger said. If he'd been startled, he recovered quickly. "How about you?" He was young, but Middlemass would not have described him as immature. The stranger had a very direct gaze, he was appraising Middlemass. He showed no signs of guilt, of being caught in the act of destroying property. This was an obvious way of disarming Middlemass, much too obvious.

"You've got a permit to destroy badger snares?"

"Yes," the stranger said. "I've got a combined licence for a garden hose, snare cutters and a colour TV set."

"I can't quite place your accent," Middlemass said.

"I take elocution lessons," the young man said. "Anything else you want to know?"

Middlemass was intrigued by this hard sell. "Only one thing. Why are you giving me the treatment?"

"I'm sorry. But these snares get up my nostrils. Who the

hell do they think they are? Any day now they'll be deporting the peasants to Australia for nicking horse dung."

"Who will?"

"The feudal fantasy lot up at Rookwood House. Laurence Adam and his merry men. Pheasant-happy fuckers."

"It costs Mr. Adam money to preserve his pheasants."

"And to let a woodland go to hell in the process? That fat-arsed money pedlar up the hill. He buys a wood and lets it strangle in ivy and wrecks the natural balance with snares and shotguns. That's nasty, that's obscene."

"I'm his guest," Middlemass said.

"I'm sorry to hear that. Sorry for you. But if you could pass on my opinions, I'd be grateful."

"Wouldn't I need to know your name?" Middlemass asked.

"Max Lawson. And you're John Middlemass?"

"Right. How did you know?"

"We'd be plunged into darkness and ignorance but for the gossip in the pub, Mr. Middlemass. Mr. Adam has one male guest and that just has to be you."

"Suppose I did my duty as a guest and told Mister Adam or his gamekeeper?"

"Make it the gamekeeper if you can. Those snares aren't legal. Not at this height."

"I wouldn't think of telling him. I was testing you. But suppose he finds out?"

"I can't wait," Max said. "Where I come from any keeper who put down snares like that would end in the nearest pond. And if he happened to kill a dog with one, his pheasantry would go up in smoke on the first dry night."

"That might also happen where I was born." Middlemass waited for the question, which did not come. "In Moravia, that was. You're not so far from home yourself?"

"Far enough," Max Lawson said.

"Living at the pub?"

"Not on your life. The landlord's okay and his wife. But they let an old duck look after the boarders. She's so bloody genteel that she hands round fingerbowls with the Cornish pasties."

Again Middlemass was intrigued. There was no such person in the Rookwood Arms. Lawson wasn't trying very hard.

"I didn't see you in the pub last night."

"I use the snug." Max said. "The dart board's there and I've got to keep fit somehow."

"And you've also got to sleep someplace." For all his talk, Lawson wasn't exactly spouting personal information.

"That's so," Max said. "I'm staying with an old friend of my family. Colonel Radford, retired. He used to be an Army padre. Don't laugh too loudly. You'll frighten the pheasants."

"I'll try to restrain myself," Middlemass said. "You must have a lot in common with a priest."

"Oh, he's not so bad," Max said. "He doesn't dish out Christianity with the cornflakes."

Middlemass hadn't heard of Colonel Radford and this intrigued him. Laurence Adam never understood why the longer-established landowners avoided him or why his tenants were as silent as moles in his presence. But he was chairman of the Rookwood Branch of the British Legion, he allowed few retired Army officers to escape him and he liked to talk about them. "Rookwood House is always open to colonels," Middlemass said. "They seem to be in strength down here."

"Too true," Max said. "You get lynched for letting the sun set on the flag. And the smell of Blanco Number 103 is something hellish."

"Blanco Number 103," Middlemass repeated exactly. "Is that the khaki-green colour?"

"I wouldn't know," Max said. "It sounds revolting enough."

"It is," Middlemass said. Conscription had been abolished in Britain for many years and no civilian of Lawson's age would define blanco so exactly. Despite his appearance, this young man was probably a soldier. Lawson's accent was also interesting. Middlemass's highly attuned ear suggested that he was doing his best to lose a public school accent, like so many young Britishers who were ashamed of the privilege their voices betrayed. A former public school boy would probably be an Army officer, not a ranker. . . .

"I haven't played darts for years," Middlemass said. It wasn't exactly usual for civilian American agents to cooperate with British military intelligence. But it was impossible. "How about a game?"

"Darts? Sure," Max said. "Any particular time?"

"Now if you like. The pub opens early."

"Soon, maybe," Max said. He waved his wire cutters. "I'm still on demolition work and I need a steady hand."

Middlemass noticed that Lawson's steady hand was shaking.

14

As HE WATCHED a dung beetle struggling to push its load up-hill, Max Lawson sympathised. He was in much the same spot himself. From the moment he arrived in Rookwood, he had been working with maximum inefficiency, trying to es-tablish that he was not suited for this work. But even Middle-mass had let him down. Max had done his level best to be rude to the investment banker and the American had retali-ated by offering him a beer and a game of darts. At times Max wondered if there was an international conspiracy to make him, a natural loudmouth and a born civilian, into a soldier and a spy. Somehow he had to convince the Fright-eners that he was endangering this operation. Somehow he had to be taken off and sent back to Aldershot for court-martial or whatever his regiment had to offer. He felt certain he could run from Aldershot, once he had given his solemn promise as an officer and a gentleman to stay and take his punishment like a man. There was no escape from Rook-wood, the Frighteners were thin on the ground, but they had an eye on him and they could move into the forest in strength, like a more virulent form of elm disease. . . .

"No primroses at this time of year," the Sky Eater said and Max noted sourly that Wainright had materialized from behind a tree, like Oberon. Wainright and the Fairy King had qualities in common.

"What were you looking for?" Major Wainright asked.

"My false nose and my beard," Max said lamely, and he was annoyed when Wainright laughed. How could he persuade the SAS to send him back to homely Aldershot in comfy chains?

"You're a born clown," Wainright said.

"Thank you, sir. I want to make the Army my career."

"We can use all sorts of people, it appears. Did Middlemass find you amusing?"

"You were watching?" Max knew that the Sky Eater was strong on field craft, but this was Eagle Scout stuff.

"Of course. You ought to be more observant. You didn't notice a thing."

"Oh, come on," Max said. "You were the third blasted oak from the right, signalling to the sycamore tree." Wainright's mouth tightened and he turned away. As Max followed, Wainright pointed with his ash stick. It was absolutely bloody typical of the Sky Eater to find the rare print of a roebuck while Max was trying to send him glibbering up the trees.

"Recognise it?" Wainright asked.

"Give me a minute, will you?" Max asked. "Pretty widely spaced . . . a vulture doing handsprings?"

"Roebuck," Wainright said. "The roe deer aren't supposed to cross railway lines but they must have done round here. I wonder if I should write to *Country Life* about it?"

"Why not the *Daily Mirror?*" Max asked. "Fascinating things happening in these woods." Wainright ignored him and followed the roe trail with Max behind him, wondering why he'd suddenly lost his gift for rudeness and why everybody was being so irrationally reasonable.

"You don't give a beetle's balls for wild life, do you?" he asked.

"Depends on what you mean by wild life." The Sky Eater was still bland. "Every infantry man must read the ground he travels and survive on what he finds."

"On roe buck?"

"Dear boy, what do they teach you in your regiment these days? Don't you know how fast a roe buck travels?"

"I've some idea."

"Or how it sidesteps? Or how dangerous it can be in the rut? Any idea how many men have been gored?"

"I can't see a roe buck goring you."

"How did you survive at Sandhurst, Max? An angry roe buck makes excellent pistol practice. Or you can snare them, then kill them with one sharp blow on the nose. They die of shock, you follow?"

"Pardon me while I puke."

"You ought to practice the nose rap, you know. Much the best way with an angry dog. They die even faster. How did you make out with Middlemass, by the way?"

"Very well," Max said. "We're having a game of darts today. Then we're getting married by special licence."

"Excellent," Wainright said. "Don't be too obviously nosey but we are rather interested in his car. It looks like a Ford Cortina Estate but his daughter drove it down here as if it were an E Type Jaguar. I wonder how?"

"Maybe she took lessons from Steve McQueen," Max said.

"Don't *lead* the conversation toward the car," Wainright said, "but if he starts talking about it himself, let him expand. You follow?"

"No," Max said. "Which insurance company are we working for?" Wainright had been lightly tracing round a roe deer rutting ring. He kept his eyes down while he hacked at

131

the ring with his stick. This was an act of violence, Wainright's equivalent of beating up old ladies.

"Rutting ring," Wainright said as if he hadn't ruined it. "You can find them as late as November although the roe rut is early, as you know. If you're going to meet Middlemass in the pub, you'd better cut along and change your gear."

"I don't think he expects me to put on a black tie and a puke suit," Max said.

"You'd better change those filthy boots."

"I've got a few more questions."

"Fire away."

"I would if I could see the target," Max said. "We're *supposed* to be guarding Middlemass."

"Supposed to be?"

"In a wood this size, and he can wander all over it."

"So?"

"So who's checking the wood for mines and booby traps?"

"I am," Wainwright said.

"On your own? And who's guarding Rookwood House?"

"I don't think that concerns you."

"No? Supposing I didn't recognise the guard and we shot it out?"

"I wish you'd handle your own affairs and let me handle mine," the major said. "We're simply the advance group. We're fairly certain Middlemass' enemies haven't arrived yet."

"No doubt they'll drop you a line," Max said. "And that reminds me. The postmistress and the postman. They're checking for exploding envelopes? Or the latest Get Well Soon cards?"

"I could explain but I won't," Wainright said. "That's security work at high level."

"Hope Middlemass doesn't end up there with it," Max

said. "You're interested in the car? But we haven't much transport, have we? Nor a fast enough car for an escort if Middlemass decides to put his boot down on the floor?"

Wainright checked his watch. Naturally he also wore a wrist compass. "I wouldn't be too sure of that," he said. "Our transport is another matter which doesn't concern you. Let's talk about something which does. We understand that Mister Middlemass is interested in the European sparrow hawk. . . ."

"Who are *we?*"

"And we hope that you'll help him to see one. The Americans call them duck hawks actually."

"They'd have to duck for this bastard keeper," Max said.

"On the motorway, off the keeper's beat."

"Oh, come on," Max said. "Helicopters keep flying over that stretch."

"Nevertheless, there is a sparrow hawk there. Grown accustomed to the helicopters as it has to cars." He gave the map reference and then pointed. "Over there, beyond that patch of sour soil with the rhododendrons."

As he developed his argument and his instructions, Max nodded miserably. When Wainright finished, he gave his last nod, walked fifteen paces then turned abruptly. The Sky Eater had vanished and he wished that he could work that trick and make the bastard disappear forever.

As he cleared the wood, he caught the whiff of a silage heap, which stank no worse than this operation. The Frighteners were usually efficient but he saw few signs of it here. This was more like an execution job, where they used few men in case the target grew suspicious and moved away too fast. . . .

Max stopped in his tracks. This was *very* like an execution job and if it was, Middlemass was the obvious target.

He had nothing more than the word of Brigadier Murray-

Strachan that Middlemass was an influential ally who had to
be guarded. There was one serious snag in his new theory.
They would not kill Middlemass without destroying the evidence and *he*, Lieutenant Lawson, was a walking piece of
evidence. Even the Frighteners drew the line somewhere,
they did not murder brother officers. . . .

Max walked slowly toward Colonel Radford's house. They
didn't need him as a contact. Why should they use an insub-
ordinate, unreliable security risk like himself when some
quiet, amenable, laboratory rat of a subaltern could have
done the job? Now he was supposed to show an interest in the
American's Ford Cortina. Obviously the car had been re-
built. Equally obviously the Frighteners could have found
out how and why with a few discreet enquiries at Ford's of
Dagenham.

The key to the front door was under a milk bottle, as
usual. Colonel Radford tried to seem casual about his old
thatched cottage, he claimed that he collected rent from the
starlings in the eaves and in the attic and his standing joke
was that only the death watch beetles held the ancient beams
together.

But Radford's joke was more suspect than the beams, for
the colonel padre was obsessionally tidy. If he had cared
about that house as he cared about his other possessions, the
beetles would have been under fire and the front door se-
curely locked.

And how about Radford himself? Why should this austere,
aesthetic priest decide to take a scruffy subaltern and a mili-
tant atheist as a casual boarder, simply to please some old
friend in the Army? Max had a quick look round. He was
certain that Radford would be out at this time of day, his
movements were as predictable as an electric hare's. The

colonel's story was that he had to exercise Barney, his retriever, but the dog was always too clean and too active when they came back.

It wasn't easy to search the cottage. Although the front door opened easily, certain drawers and cupboards did not. Besides, Colonel Radford was so methodical that he would notice if a cuff link had been moved.

Max searched for half an hour, feeling steadily more furtive and futile. At last he reached the colonel's bedroom and hesitated in the doorway. The place was so harmoniously arranged that the only thing that caught his eye was the book on the bedside table. Max picked it up and wondered again about the complex mind of David Radford, the priest whose bedside reading was *Josephus on the Jewish War*, the book that was still the most powerful argument against the possibility that Jesus had ever lived, in Max's view. . . .

A key dropped out, a mortice key, hardly the thing Radford would use as a book mark. The only mortice lock was on the garden shed and Max decided to go through the shed, then call it a day.

As he had expected, Radford's gardening tools were laid out as a lightning time-and-motion study. He looked through the shears and shovels, hoes and dibbers, rakes and trowels, then moved to the mechanical equipment.

The mechanical cultivator was not hard against the wall. Max wheeled it back and saw the blue plastic sack marked NITRO-CHALK. Radford would not have wanted anything so vulgar and inorganic to be on view. He was about to push back the mechanical cultivator when he remembered that nitro-chalk would be of no value in this garden. Inside the sack, in a lightly oiled cloth he found a submachine gun, a Sterling Paget, an assassin's dream weapon, an almost silent gun with a fire rate of 550 rounds a minute. So far as Max knew, it was still a rare weapon in the British Army and used only by the Special Air Service.

"A priest with a submachine gun," Max said to himself, "no bloody wonder he's reading about the Jewish War." He stripped the submachine gun, removed a piece, reassembled it and put it back behind the cultivator. When he'd locked the shed, he put the key in the right page on the bedside table and headed for the pub.

One of the charms of the Rookwood Arms was that it could be approached by an overgrown lane. In his wisdom, the local farmer did not cut the hedges back so that the pub approach was hidden from the intolerantly temperate and the angry wife alike. At the top of the lane the guilty drinker could look down on the pub, the car park and the road beyond, then turn back if he felt it wiser. But the hedge was rotten with ivy, not at all like the armour-plated hawthorn hedges of Thomas Hardy's time. . . .

A hand grabbed Max's ankle and he was pulled toward the ditch. As he rolled, he was temporarily blinded by the lash of hawthorn branches. He hit out with the heel of his hand and missed. As he struck out again his hand was grabbed.

"Bugger this for a tale," Sergeant Todd said. "Mud wrestling's for women."

Max rubbed his smarting eyes and stared. Todd was grinning but his face was candle coloured.

"What's the game?" Max asked.

"Patience," his platoon sergeant said. "You were bound to make for the boozer sometime."

"You've been here for hours? Why?"

"Answering the call of nature," Todd said.

Max had never seen his sergeant in civvies before. The

Harris tweed jacket looked carefully preserved but the left arm was blood stained. As Max touched it, Todd winced.

"You've been shot at?"

"Oh, no, sir," Todd said. "I was shaving me armpits and the razor slipped."

15

THE BAR AT THE ROOKWOOD ARMS opened at ten and officially closed at two thirty but the publican closed when the mood was on him for the local policeman had five villages to protect and he was a tolerant man who only dropped in to clear the bar when he felt like an afternoon pint.

And so the morning customers drank slowly and sociably, almost like Europeans, with Middlemass in their midst. When his glass was empty, the landlord drew him another pint of keg bitter without asking. Although Middlemass disliked English beer, he drank it at the Rookwood Arms, knowing that a man who never drank beer in a Wessex pub was not a man to be trusted.

"We haven't even seen your daughter yet," the publican said. Middlemass was glad he'd dropped in there before this as part of his casual bluff.

"You will and there are other Americans around. I've got a hunch."

"Never. I promised you, didn't I? If a Yank pokes his snout into Rookwood, I'll let you know. If you want to dodge them on holiday, that's your business."

"Like Lawson," Middlemass said.

"Like who?"

"Max Lawson. A young fellow. He plays darts, he tells me but I haven't seen him."

"Oh, him?" the publican looked at the farm manager, then they both examined the ceiling.

"I've asked him around for a beer," Middlemass said.

"That's your affair, Mister Middlemass," the publican said.

"Living with a clergyman. He's got to be bored."

The farm manager sniggered. "That what he told you?" the publican asked. "The nearest vicar's at Tolchester and he's got the five parish churches to look after. He's been known to have as many as seven people in Rookwood Church of a Sunday. That was at Christmas, of course."

"I mean a retired Army priest. A padre. Colonel Radford."

"So Radford's a padre, is he?" the farm manager asked.

"You didn't know?"

"Not much chance to find out," the publican said. "The house was standing empty until Radford turned up. He'd two furniture vans, London registrations, and maybe five men to help him move in . . . and not one of them had his collar turned the wrong way round." The publican checked that the only stranger in the bar was out of hearing. "Next thing young what's-his-name Lawson shows up. Tell you what I think. Retired Army padre? Rhubarb. He's a rich old queen and the young bloke's his boyfriend."

Middlemass had information to process but that didn't stop him lying on his feet. "I got the impression Lawson's deeply religious. The padre is instructing him, I suppose." He didn't know much about the Anglican religion but he was banking on the others knowing less. A solemn silence fell.

"You a religious man yourself, Mister Middlemass?" the farm manager asked at last.

"I used to think so, but now . . . I don't know . . . I've got

140

doubts. That's why I want to talk to Lawson." The pub was the only place that was relatively safe and a religious discussion was the last thing the locals would want to know about or interrupt. He looked down the lane. "He shouldn't be long," Middlemass said. "All right if we talk in the snug?"

His instinct told him Lawson could be useful, his reason warned him he was playing Russian roulette with a fully loaded revolver. As always, though, he backed his hunch.

Max checked on Todd's arm and satisfied himself that it was only a flesh wound, already healing. Then he sat in cover by the ditch.

"Dreaming?" Todd asked. "Or just growing moss on your arse?"

"It doesn't figure," Max said. "They treat me like a royal lunatic and they try to kill you. Something's missing."

"Yeah, a jar or two of my blood. You want me to go through it again?"

"I think I can bear it."

"Right. You ring me and you're dead pissed but you tell me to scarper. So I natter with the orderly-room sergeant on the quiet and it turns out that everybody in our old platoon is in for a bit of a shock. Soon as their leave's over, they're getting posted overseas again and out of the regiment. Not one of them's going to the same place as his mates. They're getting scattered from Hong Kong to the Caribbean. What you reckon?"

"Two things," Max said. "The Parachute Brigade wants to forget about the sergeant major's death. No witnesses, so no court-martial."

"And?"

"If anything happens to you or me, none of the platoon will know for years. Did you kill the sergeant major?"

"Sure," Todd said. "Asking for it, wasn't he?" He stared at Max, picking his teeth with a nail. Lawson knew he was growing callous. Todd's admission that he had killed the sergeant major did not trouble him as much as he expected, it was simply the last piece in the old puzzle and the new one was far more complicated. . . .

"How about the Redcap officer?"

"He wanted you to run for it," Max said.

"Check. And I was daft enough to do it. That's what they wanted, right? I would vanish and be posted as a deserter for the next thirty years. Nobody would know for sure whether I was living it up in Bury, Lancs or a nice big hunk of fertiliser, six feet down."

"You lost your nerve?" Max asked. "Doesn't sound like you."

Todd had evaded that point before but he was tiring. He had moved too far and too fast for a wounded man without sufficient food or sleep. "Oh, yeah. One thing I forgot to tell you," he said. "There was a bit of a knees-up in the sergeants' mess and the orderly-room sergeant asked me where you were and how you were making out.

" 'He's at Rookwood,' I says, 'and he don't seem too hilariously happy.' "

" 'Rookwood?' asks the orderly-room sergeant. 'That's funny. There's not an Army camp for miles and miles round there. Last time it was used was years ago. The Frighteners were down there on an exercise.' "

" 'Exercise?' I says. 'Those bastards only got one exercise and that's using other people's guts for chest expanders.' " Todd trailed off.

Max was beginning to understand. "What happened to the very helpful sergeant?"

"He got posted. Hardly time to pack his kit."

"And there were Frightener sergeants in your mess?"

"Yeah, well there's always a few of them at Aldershot, that's what I forgot."

"But that wouldn't make you go on the trot? You don't panic that easily."

"Well, the chance came up see? Mate of mine was doing moonlight."

"Moving out his furniture without paying the rent? Very convenient. Quite a lucky coincidence?"

"Yeah, wasn't it?" So I kept my head down then nipped into the back of the furniture van sharp and went up to London. Chance I couldn't miss, see?" He was aggrieved by Max's reluctance to buy the story entirely. "That you going into a trance again? It's me that's spilled the blood."

"I was just thinking over your story," Max said. "You left Aldershot in a furniture van. You got to Soho and you thought you were safe. . . ."

"And nearly in bed with a tart."

"Before a gunman in civvies took a pot at you?"

"We been over all that."

"Not all of it. The Frighteners don't often miss."

"They didn't," Todd said. "It just so happened that this tart got atween me and the line of fire."

"That was another thing you forgot to mention."

"I was waiting for you to ask," Todd said. "You don't think all this blood's my own? My fuel guage would be at nothing if it was."

Max examined Todd's jacket. Then he sighed, peeled off his anorak and handed it over. His sweater would pass for outdoor clothing. "You didn't use her as a shield, by any chance?"

"What do you take me for?" Todd asked. "I come here to stand by you. . . ."

"You do what?"

"I come here to warn you. I owe it to you, right?"

"You came here because you'd no place else to go," Max said, "and because you're a cunning turd and you reckon this is the last place they'd look for you." He was grinning, though, and Todd responded wanly. "But you couldn't know the Frighteners were here. So what were you doing in that ditch?"

Todd's professional pride was touched. "I was looking for you, wasn't I? And who comes past but Prick Nose Prentice?"

Max cursed himself and his stupidity. If Wainright was around, his batman and bodyguard Prentice, the trooper with that unfortunate nose would have to be here, too, although the Sky Eater would keep his thug-in-waiting out of sight. . . .

"You getting hazy again?" Todd asked.

"Maybe. How long can you last out in this ditch?"

"How do you mean? Any idea how long I was on my chuff in Borneo with both my ankles broken? Days and nights, nights and bloody days."

"I'll be as fast as I can but you'll have time to bury that jacket," Max said. His mind was clearing. If they'd tried to kill Todd, they'd do the same for him. They could even justify the act. Todd was a murderer and he was an accessory to the deed. It would be simpler to remove them than to stain the Army's reputation with a court-martial. He had been proved wrong, the Army would and did attempt to kill their own people on the quiet.

On the other hand, it would not occur to them that Max and Todd could hit back. Not in their worst nightmares would they imagine that a brother officer, however dishonoured, would piss upon his country's flag rather than play the ritual goat for sacrifice. Max could imagine such "treachery" quite easily. In his book of quotations, patriotism was the last refuge of lunatics not scoundrels.

Middlemass would still be in the pub. He did not know what the American had done to earn an execution but this was no time to worry about the morals of a cobelligerent.

"Sweeney, we're going to have to make a dodgey bargain with a man in this deeper than we are."

"Nobody could be that deep without the flowers growing on him."

"He's still breathing and he's rich."

"Show me his money and I'll sign."

"He's an American." Todd's views on Americans were widely known.

"I might've guessed. There had to be a catch."

16

MIDDLEMASS NEEDED no instruction in darts. He began with a double top and ended the game the same way. "Pure luck," he said.

"You're going to need it."

"Another game, you mean?"

"Not just yet," Max said, "I've got a problem. Maybe you can help."

Middlemass collected the darts and threw them in a narrow group around the bull. "Advice from me? When you're living with a padre?"

"This is more of a secular problem," Max said. "Supposing you wanted to guard an important visitor in Rookwood?"

"Against what?"

"Arab terrorists," Max said. "How would you set about it?"

"Well, I'd keep a sharp eye out for sandals," Middlemass said. "And I'd search the woods. They might try to camouflage their camel concentrations."

"Good thinking," Max said. "You wouldn't simply have a few gunmen from the Special Air Service keeping an eye on your guest?"

"Not if I wanted him to live," Middlemass said. Hope was rising again, he couldn't see why the enemy should feed him such information. The presence of the SAS explained a lot. "Is that helpful?"

"Very," Max said. "Now, put yourself in this visitor's place."

"I'm not good at imagining things."

"Try," Max said. "You're the visitor, for the sake of argument. And a stranger starts asking awkward questions about your car? How would you feel?"

Middlemass was trying to place the darts by throwing them underhand. "I think I'd get suspicious," he said. "I might even tell the locals and they could go to the police."

"And how would the police react?"

"Slowly," Middlemass said. "They'd forget all about it until something happened to the American."

"Which American?" Max asked.

"The one being guarded against the camel raids. Then the police would remember the man interested in the car."

"You think the police would suspect him?"

"I'm certain."

"Fine. Mister Middlemass, I'd like to ask you questions about your Ford Cortina Estate. Or is it an E-Type Jaguar in drag?"

Middlemass's reason told him this was a trap. His hunch was that Lawson was levelling. Even if it weren't, he might use Lawson before Lawson used him.

"Why not take a ride in it?" Middlemass said. "My daughter wants to go to Tolchester. Come with us."

Max borrowed the darts and demonstrated how badly he could play when he wasn't concentrating. "I know another fellow who wants to leave. And he's wounded."

The bullhorns sounded in Middlemass's mind. This second

man was an unknown quantity. "I'd need to know more about him," he said.

"First-class references," Max said, "he's a marksman and he's a signals-and-explosives expert. He hates the Army worse than I do and he's a murderous git. My old platoon sergeant, it so happens."

"You mean murderous?"

"I couldn't give you his score. Neither could he. His shooting's better than his arithmetic. He killed one of ours and I hid the evidence. That's *one* of the reasons the Army doesn't love us any longer."

"Is he badly wounded?"

"No, and he heals faster than a worm without a tail."

"Who shot him?"

"The SAS and he doesn't like bearing grudges, he'd rather settle them."

Middlemass sat beneath the dart board and ran his hand around his chin. "It sounds as if his Army doesn't understand him."

"They could even have underestimated him. It's a habit they have."

"Institutions like the Army, they lack soul," Middlemass said. "Like large business corporations. They don't encourage individual talents. This man needs another chance."

"That's it. A fresh start. We all need that. Take the padre I'm staying with. He's lost his faith in people. He's so suspicious that he's got a Sterling Paget submachine gun hidden in his fertiliser. That gun kills quietly. The only sound is when the bullets hit the body."

"A muscular Christian, is he?" Middlemass was not unduly surprised about Colonel Radford, but he still didn't see why the enemy should feed him useful facts. "Give me time to pick up my daughter. Where can I meet you?"

"A hundred yards up the lane," Max said. "When you stop, I'll show you something strange. A roe deer print."

"Close to the pub?"

"Roebucks get thirsty, no?" Max said.

"That a hint?" Middlemass collected the glasses, went to the bar and came back with two more pints. "Suppose you're telling the truth?" he asked Max.

"Just suppose."

"You'd be crazy to trust me," Middlemass said.

"You can't be any worse than the SAS," Max said. "They ought to be remustered as the Royal Hearse Guards."

"So how do you hope to live?"

"By getting the hell out of here with you. As fast as you can shift. Before they realize I'm too old for their fairy stories."

"Such as?"

Max sampled his beer. "I wouldn't want to bore you," he said. "Tell me your problems."

"Why not?" Middlemass reasoned that he needn't tell Max anything his enemies wouldn't know. Even then he kept to the basic facts.

"Bloody hell," Max said. "You think big, don't you? And so you took these tides of men into your hands and wrote your will across the sky in stars."

"You don't mind?" Middlemass asked.

"You've got to be joking. All my life I've been trying to put a rocket up authority's arse. My only ambition. And you've got it all worked out."

"I thought I had," Middlemass said. "Before your people snatched Walters."

"Not my people. Them. The coffin soldiers. Anyhow, you haven't lost yet."

"I hope not." He'd been so close to winning but with the closing letters gone, the game was wide open. One of the

150

letters was for the backers in Zurich and his enemies had only to use stolen stationery from Middlemass' London office and forge his signature on an infuriatingly casual letter to that smug slug of a Swiss banker announcing that Middlemass didn't want his money after all.

Another put-down could be sent in place of the letter to the Japanese sponsors in Osaka. This second forged answer would probably be phrased in immaculate Japanese and decorated with graceful regrets like flowers crushed between the pages. Their letter to the Sultan of Doha would need more skill, but Middlemass was aware of the passionate Western involvement with the Arab world and its devious approaches to thought. A truly bright Arabist could employ the variations in written Arabic that the people of Doha alone used. If he were sufficiently sharp, the forger could load his reply with "unintentional" insults and ruin his standing with the Sultan for ever. Middlemass hardly considered sending telegrams or telephoning. His telegrams would be blocked and he would certainly not get through to Osaka or the Sultan of Doha by telephone. Once they had dispatched their forged replies and ensured an especially fast delivery, the opposition would make certain that he couldn't make contact.

"The main thing is to shift," Max said. "While I'm still supposed to be checking on your car. Before the Sky Eater knows I've changed sides."

"Who?"

"The SAS leader. A pistol-happy prick." He gave a potted biography of Major Wainright. "He seems to know a lot about you, especially your interest in wildlife."

"Anything in particular?"

"Sparrow hawks. He's heard you wanted to see sparrow hawks hunting along this stretch of the motorway at dawn, to keep away from gamekeepers. They're scarce here nowadays."

"How would he know I was interested?"

"He's chummy with Adams, your host."

"Adam," Middlemass said.

"Oh, yeah, Adam. He even looks like a period fireplace."

"You're sure he knows Adam?"

"He says so."

This was the second time he'd heard about the sparrow hawk and the first man to mention it had been Adam.

"Very interesting." Middlemass said.

"Fascinating. Look, I'm the local charity collector to save our feathered friends. I've even run the wild bird hospital on the Hammersmith flyover. But when do we get out of this place for good?"

"We don't," Middlemass said. "I'll fix your friend's arm. Then we'll talk, when I can trust you."

"I'm trusting you. Who you reckon's the bigger mug?"

"And I'll tell everybody in this bar I'm taking Shona and you to Tolchester," Middlemass said. "If we're not back this evening, they'll want to know why."

17

SHONA WAS IN THE WALLED GARDEN, walking through the smallest greenhouse. As Middlemass approached, she stopped in front of the chrysanthemums, intriguing him. Shona disliked chrysanthemums and the chances were she was unaware of them, even of their smell. She was not exactly fond of greenhouses either, she would be using this only as a place to shut out Rookwood while she thought.

She kept staring through the flowers, she did not see him, and he found her stare disquieting until he understood. He had last seen that look when he caught his own naked expression in an unexpected mirror. Shona's eyes were his eyes and he had not known that until now. But it was a breach of privacy to look at an unarmed face, he tapped on the glass.

"Yes, Dad?" She sounded petulant, a child jolted from a dream.

"You wanted to be involved in this business, so you're involved." He told her no more about Max Lawson and the wounded man than she needed to know, but he told her too much.

"You sure this isn't some kind of trap?" Shona asked. "This man Lawson cutting badger snares. Doesn't that sound like he was claiming to be your soulmate?"

"Perhaps," Middlemass said, "but we'll know for sure soon enough. He was very rude."

"It fits, Dad. That's how to impress you."

"You ought to know, Shona."

"And they're soldiers? How did the British Army get into the act?"

"That's another thing I want to know. Are you changing your clothes?"

"No, I don't think so. The Queen doesn't throw her garden parties at Tolchester, does she? Just one or two other things I have to know, though . . ."

"No time now."

"No time, no deal," she said and she walked back into the greenhouse.

"What is this? Blackmail?"

"I don't see it that way," she said. "Why would two British soldiers help *you*?"

"Because they figure their army's going to . . . erase them."

"So they've signed a separate peace? They must think you're in the same spot. And you are, aren't you?"

Middlemass considered lying then decided not to waste his time.

"Yes."

"I don't get it. Why go out of your way to get killed?"

"How often are you going to ask?"

"Until the answer comes up. You never expected to make fifty, did you? Now every year's going to be the last?"

"Who told you? Otsch Gellner?"

"What does it matter how I know? I *know*."

"You'll be all right," he said. "I've made provisions. . . ." Her expression was enough to make him stop.

"I've got to get some things from my room," he said. "And . . ."

154

". . . and I'll come with you, Dad."

In his room Middlemass opened the elaborate locks on the trunk and checked over his medical supplies.

"This thing you've got about wild animals, Dad. You'd kill people before you'd kill them."

"Why not?" he asked. "Men, they're the real predators, aren't they? They're destroying the environment for every other animal and they never give it a thought."

"That's high-flying stuff, Dad. Isn't it because you'd rather have been born a peregrine or something?"

Middlemass didn't answer, he was examining a suit intended for Todd.

"Then that dog you aimed at with an airgun. You didn't think you'd hit it but you did."

Middlemass packed a blanket and the suit in a bag but his hands weren't functioning exactly, he had trouble with the zip. "How do you know all that? About the peregrine? And the dog?"

"You don't remember the peregrine?"

"No," he said. "And I'd have remembered if I'd told you."

"You would have remembered if you'd told me when you were sober," she said. "But when I was young, when you were fighting with . . . her, you used to come into my bedroom after you'd killed a bottle. Then you'd talk to me. You don't remember?"

"No," he said, "and don't tell me any more."

It was years since he'd talked about peregrines. He'd dropped the subject when those predators vanished from the eastern seaboard of North America. But he had always envied peregrines and their eyes, which were larger, heavier and twice as able as any man's. He'd never forgotten the falcon he'd watched, staring at him like a slate-blue stone, as if he weren't there, for the peregrine had no fear of a distant unarmed man. Once he'd watched a pair of them, stooping out of the sun like First War fighter pilots. . . .

It fitted. Lawrence Adam had talked about a sparrow hawk and called it a duck hawk, which was a lousy name for a peregrine. In the past he might well have talked to Adam about hawks, but no one would expect him to believe there were peregrines round Rookwood. There were very few left in England and they were choosy where they lived. The peregrine did not deign to hunt too far from a shingle-bottomed stream with no less than nine inches of water and no more than twelve for its daily bath before it started quest-ing. Rookwood was mostly on chalk and singularly dry. There could be sparrow hawks around, but not by the high-ways in any numbers. Kestrels perhaps, but not sparrow hawks. The sparrow hawk and the highway connection couldn't be accidental.

As he replaced his wrecked transmitter in the trunk, ex-actly as he'd found it, he remembered how proud Walters had described stealing that set from the British Army. . . .

The SAS, the coffin soldiers, as Lawson had called them. They were bound to have a transmitter that would serve his purpose.

18

Max wandered along the hedgerow, stopped close to Todd and bent to examine an imaginary print. "Sweeney?"

"Yes, dear."

"When you hear the car stop, wait until you're shielded, then get into the back and under the blanket."

"You've made a deal with this American, then? You reckon that's safe?"

"It makes us traitors. I told you."

"Gimme time to have a quiet cry. What I mean is can we trust him, like?"

"Maybe not. Would you rather make a deal with the Frighteners? Or the sergeant major's widow?"

"We could go it alone."

"You've tried that. And the car's coming." Max got up, dusted himself and casually waved down the Ford.

Middlemass got out, followed by his daughter. Her worn jeans and ragged Mexican blanket were not ideally inconspicuous, the Rookwood social climbers were bound to follow her movements with malicious interest, but Max hardly noticed her clothes. He stared into her eyes, blinked, stared again, then dropped his eyes.

"Shona, this is Mr. Lawson."

"Oh," Max said. She held out a hand and he held it too long. "My name's Lawson."

"So I understand," Shona said.

"Did you say *you'd* something to show *me?*" Middlemass was annoyed by her obvious hostility.

"Sorry? Oh, yes. Certainly. Absolutely." Max led them to the rear of the car. As they grouped themselves between Todd and the road, Max pointed down at nothing in particular. "Would you say that was a roe print?"

Middlemass bent and drew a fair imitation of a roe print with his fingers, turning slowly to complete the circle, shielding Todd from the road. "Think so," he said, "too small for a fallow. Strange, isn't it? You'd think their numbers would be going down but they're moving into the south of England all the time. You like roe deer, Mr. Lawson?"

"They're always being hunted. I sympathise."

"Come and look, Shona," Middlemass said.

"I can see from here," she said, leaning casually on the tailgate and closing it. "Talking about moving, when do the shops close in Tolchester?"

"Did you say Tolchester?" Max asked inanely, looking at Shona again.

"You want a lift? Jump in."

Max slid into the rear seat and stared at the back of her neck as they set off. Shona Middlemass didn't look like her father, but she seemed to have inherited his nerve.

"I'm new at this game, Dad," she said, "but was all that additional dialogue really necessary? Nobody could be listening."

"They might have been watching. Are you all right in the back?" Middlemass didn't believe that a thug like Todd could be involved in a double bluff.

"Great," Todd said. "Wake me when we get there, will you?"

"Another comedian," Middlemass said. "It seems to run in your regiment."

"He means it," Max said. "But he doesn't snore too loudly. I wonder if Wainright will follow us?"

"He will." Middlemass braked abruptly, snatched a newspaper, opened the hood, worked swiftly, then slammed the lid. When they took off, he drove faster.

"You wanted to know about the car," he said to Max. "Are you mechanically inclined?"

"I don't understand the principle of the wheel. Sergeant Todd does, though. Sweeney?" Todd ignored him.

"I'll give you the facts and you can screw them up, it'll sound more natural," Middlemass said. "The Ford has been fitted with a turbo-charged three-litre V6 engine. Specially assembled, balanced and with a modified camshaft. Large valves, fuel injection and exhaust driven turbo-charger. Will you remember some of that?"

"Some."

"It should have a top speed of a hundred and forty. But the special low back axle ratio restricts that to a hundred and thirty. It does zero to sixty time of six point five seconds. When you mentioned the E-type Jaguar, you weren't far off."

"*Now* you tell me," Shona said.

"You weren't supposed to drive the car or go anywhere near my London office."

"I wanted to see it while it was still there," Shona said.

"She's also a comedian, Mr. Lawson. You want to know about the disc brakes, the special shock absorbers and so on?"

"I've felt them. But the engine's in trouble, isn't it?"

"Yes, and the trouble's going to be more spectacular, soon. I want the opposition out in front."

159

"Before we blow up?"

"We won't. I've only jammed paper in the air intake."

On the next series of hairpin bends, they heard the Mini. As it closed on them, Major Wainright braked abruptly, almost hit them, then swung past.

Wainright slowed, then began to race ahead. "My boss the Sky Eater."

"He doesn't seem so happy on the ground."

"Or maybe Mr. Lawson wants it that way," Shona said. "Maybe that's part of the plan."

"I've only got one plan," Max said. "To retire at twenty-one. On account of good health."

19

THE AUTUMN DROUGHT had lasted for so long that even farmers had stopped wanting one kind of weather on one field and another climate on the next. Although the caravan site's holiday makers had gone and it was mainly occupied by construction workers and their families, the café still had metal tables and plastic chairs outside.

"Sorry about the biscuits," Max said but Shona ignored him, keeping an eye on her father in the garage. "And the weather. Every foreign visitor's entitled to muffin men calling through the yellow fog."

"You ever stop being facetious?" she asked.

"Sometimes. But it's like being rude," he said. "It's contagious."

"I don't mean to be rude. Not to you in particular."

"I understand," Max said, "you've got to keep in practice."

"So now we're quits. Will you stop staring at me?"

"I was only looking," he said. "Want me to turn my back?"

"You were staring. And these clothes, they're all I've got. Nothing worth buying round here. You fancy me in a tweed suit with a double strand of pearls?"

"I'd fancy you in anything." He waved toward the campsite guard dog. "Even in that choke lead."

161

"A choke lead might be more in your line." Her hair was unfashionably short for England, her eyes were half the face, he wanted the bickering to stop.

"I don't need a spare," he said. "My collar and my chain lead, they're hanging in my kennel back at Aldershot."

" 'The home of the British Army,' " she said. "That's what it says on the signs, I drove through Aldershot on the way down."

"Then you lost your way," he said. "Like I lost mine a long time ago."

"You have to volunteer for the British Army, don't you? And volunteer again for parachuting? And again to join an independent scouting company?"

"That's right," he said, silently cursing Todd for letting his tongue flap when they were settling him in a nearby caravan. "Hawkeye the Hood, that's me. Better not turn your back."

"So long as my father doesn't."

"That's right. Todd shot himself to make it look authentic. We're not armed. Your father is."

"He's got a gun? You're crazy."

"Usually but not this time," Max said. "I saw the bulge." He inclined his head toward Middlemass talking to the garage manager, who had defeat in his eye and dandruff on his collar.

As Shona rose, Max shook his head. "You know what he said. The car's in trouble and it's going to stay in trouble as long as he can keep it that way. Until Sweeney's recovered from your father's nursing. You and I stay here in case anybody's watching."

"It was your idea to come to this place," Shona said.

"That's right. I've been thinking about caravan sites ever

162

since I thought of running for it. But it wasn't my idea to fix the car."

As she looked toward her father again, he caught her reflection in the café window. The short hair, the great eyes in the tiny face, the long pointed collar of her shirt made her look like a brilliant schoolgirl. "What's so interesting about that window?" she asked.

"Your face, the reflection." he said. "I was thinking you looked like Nefertiti."

"Oh, come on, she's dead. Is it all right if I go to . . . what do you call it? The powder room?"

"That's what we always call it," Max said, "so don't light too many matches."

Middlemass came over when she left, as Max had expected. He hadn't cared for the drift of Middlemass' thought in the last hour, he expected the worst and it came.

"Something I want to ask you. Your specialist signalling sets. Very small? Easy to carry and simple to operate. With a range of a thousand miles or so?"

"Less than that," Max said.

"But I could signal to Switzerland?" If he could get a message through to Zurich, to be passed to Doha and Osaka before the forged letters arrived, there was still a chance.

"Switzerland? Easily." Max said.

Fortunately the emergency radio link with Zurich had been Middlemass's own idea and he had not told Harry Walters why he had needed the radio transmitter that had been sabotaged. Middlemass had learned always to keep something back, even from his closest contact. . . .

"Tell me a little more about those transmitters." Max did his best.

"Perfect," Middlemass said.

"For what?" Max asked. "If I'm on your wavelength, you want to nick an Army signalling set. Any idea how well they're guarded?"

"I can guess. But your Frightener friends must have one."

"You're not serious? You don't mean to take a set from them?"

"I'm serious," Middlemass said. "What's the unofficial motto of your regiment?"

" 'Do unto others before they do unto you.' " Max's reply was so automatic it disturbed him.

"And how many Frighteners at Rookwood?" Middlemass asked. "Two? Three?"

"But their support's not far away," Max said. "The main SAS mob, they're in a pub, masquerading as a rugby side."

"A what?"

"Football team," Max said, "but they're better at kicking than passing. You mean to signal Switzerland to bring on Spider Man and Hulk?"

Middlemass looked sympathetic but Max remembered that look on the face of Brigadier Murray-Strachan. "You've got a better plan, Max?"

"Yes, sure. You took me for a drive, your car broke down and that's all. Todd can slip away from here. If you still want to sweat it out, that's your worry. I'll come back with you. Then I'll scarper when I get the chance."

Middlemass shrugged. It was a Central European gesture, implying that the situation was desperate but not serious. "I thought we agreed you've been sent down here as bait?"

"We did. It doesn't make sense any other way."

"So you won't get away alone. Whatever happens to the fish, the bait usually gets killed."

"I feel like a maggot already," Max said, "I'm really glad I asked you for advice."

"You might be, one day. Can you spike Colonel Radford's submachine gun?"

"I've done it."

"You don't usually sound so confident."

"I had my own shooter spiked once," Max said. "Out in Arabia. So I know a bit about it now."

"Fine," Middlemass checked his watch. "They've done almost everything to that car except empty the ashtray. We'll have to move, soon."

"Hope we make it to Rookwood."

"We'll make it," Middlemass said. "You once had a gun spiked. I was once captured on a road. Now I know a bit about tailing and ambushes." He looked up as Shona joined them. "You all right?"

"I'll survive," she said. "They don't need to bug *this* place. The ladies room, it's great for listening in. When were you captured on a road, Dad?"

"I had an agreement with your mother. If she promised not to sell god to you, I wouldn't talk about the past. You think I should keep that promise?"

"If you can," she said. "Why do the British want you so badly? I can understand the Americans but why the British?"

"I'm not too sure myself," Middlemass said. "Flattering, isn't it?" He pushed money toward Max. "Go to camp reception, will you? Tell them our friend's feeling better. We're checking out when the car's ready. We won't be staying after all."

"Supposing Todd wants to stay?" Max asked. "Especially when he hears about the Desperate Dan routine to snatch War Department property."

"He'll come," Middlemass said. He forced the money on

Max. "That's for the caravan site," he said, "it doesn't affect your amateur standing."

"You wouldn't ask him to earn a living at it, would you Dad?"

"Not with you around." He was pleased but surprised by her shift of sympathy. "Go with him, will you? Flutter your eyelashes at the camp boss and he'll forget to ask questions."

"Maybe I'd better go alone," Max said. "Your daughter doesn't reckon much by my performance."

"I'll play along," she said. "I got straight A's in acting."

She walked behind him, round shouldered, arms folded across her Mexican blanket, a dejected squaw. "You've acted?" he asked.

"Some. At school. Eugene O'Neill, you know? One foot in Greek drama and the other in pig swill. Incest, near incest, or anyway let's keep sex inside the family. But this is a different part."

"At least your father isn't acting," Max said. "He makes up a story then he believes it, then he makes it come true."

"Dad? You're kidding," Shona said. "He's always playing a part. Want to guess who?"

"Alcibiades?" Max asked, "Raleigh? Some bold black-hearted bastard?'

"You get the drift," she said, "but you're a few years off. His idea of a man was St. John Philby. An Englishman."

"Some Englishman."

In the First World War, Philby had crossed the Empty Quarter of Arabia instead of bringing the Saudis into war against the Turks. He had thrown away the chance to shorten the conflict and to outshine Lawrence of Arabia, reckoning he had better things to do. Then Philby had persuaded the Saudis to sell their oil to the Americans rather than to his own country. By the second World War, he was trying to convince King Ibn Saud that the Allies had no hope of winning the war. And he had fathered Kim Philby, the most distinguished British traitor of our time.

"I don't need to point out the similarities, do I?" Shona asked.

"I get the drift."

"He used to let his tongue flap when he was drunk. Jesus Christ. Imagine."

"No, don't," he said. "Think of something else."

"Like why you're letting him talk to Todd alone?"

"They're going to bargain. Money for blood," Max said. "I just don't want to know."

The children's skipping rhyme carried from the caravans:

> *Ipper dipper dation*
> *My operation*
> *How many people waiting at the station?*
> *Or how many stitches will you have?*

"If I were superstitious that song would worry me," Shona said. "And I'm very superstitious."

20

MIDDLEMASS KNOCKED on the caravan door. "Come in," Todd said. As Middlemass pushed the door, it was wrenched open, he stumbled in and saw Todd with a knife in his hand. "Sorry, squire. But you might have been a foreigner or something."

Middlemass lightly touched the point of the blue steel blade. "A fighting knife?" he asked. "I didn't know your Army issued them anymore."

"They don't," Todd said. "I borrowed it from a bloke in Dad's Army. I like antiques, see."

"I had a knife like that once. In the war."

Todd looked shocked. "You were in the war? Poor old bastard. You oughta be in a wheelchair."

As he sat down, Middlemass checked the level in the whisky bottle. "Knives and whisky. You like the good things in life, don't you?"

"Maybe. But I never got done for marking a man and I never get a hangover."

"I envy you." Middlemass' sarcasm was obvious even to Todd. They both knew that this was too often the sign of an alcoholic. "I've come to organise your packing."

"Thanks all the same, nob, but I like it here," Todd said.

"Cushy old caravan, this is. Better than lotsa hotels that charge an extra quid for the cobwebs."

Middlemass took out his wallet and dropped it on the table.

"Put your folding stuff away, will you, whack? That kinda wad makes me nervous."

Middlemass left the money where it was.

"Last time I saw that amount of notes, we was playing Monopoly," Todd said. "What have I gotta do for that lot? Murder the Pope?"

"I can't talk about plans until I know where you stand."

"And I don't pick up the poppy until I know what I gotta do."

Middlemass turned the only chair around and sat down, leaning heavily on the chair back. It had been a long day and there was more work still to do. "Suppose I told you and you chickened out, then got captured?" he asked.

Todd had no answer and Middlemass searched his memory for suitable British Army slang. "Come on," he said. "We're all up Shit Creek together and we've lost the paddle."

"Stuff the paddle, I'd rather have a shooter if it's all the same to you."

Middlemass remembered Colonel Radford's submachine gun. "Would a Sterling Paget do?" he asked.

Todd spat deliberately into the bucket. "Yeah, fine," he said. "But how do you get it? Do you ankle up to a Frighteners' arms store? And say 'Excuse me, colour sergeant, but I'm a white fig from Black Power. Shove us over a silent submachine gun, will you, colour sergeant?' "

Middlemass waved to the whisky bottle. "You're still two drinks under par," he said. "I hope that's the right brand. All they had in the camp store."

"Cat's piss," Todd said. "You can stuff your whisky. I'm not working in the dark."

Middlemass counted out a few bills and handed them over. "Good-bye, sergeant," he said. "That money will keep you for a week or two. Best of luck, sergeant. You could be free for days, maybe weeks."

Todd ignored the money and swigged at the whisky. "Hellish," he said, "if only I could get some berk to take my first belt of whisky for me, morning, noon and night."

Middlemass placed the small bills on the table and headed for the door. "Sit down," Todd said, "I'm in. But I gottan idea it's gonta be rough. I'll need more money than you got in that roll."

"You'll get it."

"And a bent passport?"

"I can get one for you," Middlemass said. "What'll we call you? Peter Roberts?"

"You wouldn't make it John Thomas, could you?" Todd asked. "I haven't had a bang for days. Soon as I asked my old woman questions, she started to ration me." He took a longer swig. "How did *you* get into this?" he asked. "You with all that folding money? How come you're up Shit Creek with Lawson and me?"

"I killed a man," Middlemass said, "what did you do?"

21

THE ROOKWOOD ARMS piano was being milked by an elderly
dairyman with badly fitting teeth. While he ran through his
repertoire from *Stranger in the Night* to *Be Kind to Your
Web-Footed Friends,* the other locals crowded the domino
players against the men who were arguing about the use of
cow manure on dahlias. The younger farm workers with long
hair and the latest line in flairs they'd seen on television,
were willingly being driven close to Shona. They waited and
watched to see which one of them would be bold enough to
draw her into an intense conversation on the winter corn
prices or how many tractors he had bent that year. This corner of the pub was dark but lit by lechery.

Middlemass, meanwhile, was listening to the landlord on
the dangers of the new fertilisers taking the taste from the
barley and the ale.

"Relax," Middlemass said. "They like your beer. Look at
the crowd. Just about every local except the gamekeeper."

The landlord scowled and used undue force on the beer
pump handle. "He don't come and I wouldn't want him," he
said. "Right bastard he is and no mistake. Two dogs and

three cats missing from this village in a twelvemonth. Somebody'll snare him, one of these fine days. By the knackers, with any luck."

"Somebody must love him someplace," Middlemass said.

"All I know is, he's got no friends round here. Nothing's safe from him that walks or crawls or flies."

Middlemass paid for his round and bought the landlord a drink. "One thing he can't shoot, the hawks on the highway. They're off his beat, aren't they?"

The landlord counted out the change. "Hawks on the motorway, you mean? Well, I've heard tell of that, but not round here. You don't think he'd let a hawk live, even on a motorway? Not him, not if he had to patrol that road with antiaircraft pom poms." As he was called away to serve another customer, Middlemass carried a drink across to Shona and waited until the young men drifted off.

"Don't look so worried," he said.

"I'm *not* worried," she said but the rings under her eyes were breaking through the makeup before Max wandered in, bought himself a pint, then drifted over.

"Wainright buy your story?" Middlemass asked.

"Think so. All the crap about the car, anyway. We've got company."

Middlemass nodded. "The young man with the gray suit?"

"He's one of the reserves. The rugby football side I was telling you about."

"We'll keep him on the bench," Middlemass said. "Drink slowly and get me one in your next round. Sit it out as long as you can before you notice that I've vanished. If the rugby player leaves, phone the house. Let it ring three times. But don't talk."

Middlemass headed for the lavatory, left by the door to the street and set off for Rookwood. On the way he stopped by the cattleshed and lit a cigarette. As his match flared, the pheasants panicked in the trees around him.

"What you want them to do?" Todd asked from the dark. "They don't lay eggs this time of year."

"You all right?"

"Certainly," Todd said. "Born in a manger, wasn't I?"

At Rookwood House Middlemass phoned the pub, then settled in the library to run through the details of the long night and longer day ahead. The idea of the highway and the wildlife around it suggested an overplanned ambush, the work of some rigid military mind; it did not sound like a Matthew Sleet plan. But there was bound to be confusion between the Americans and the British. Middlemass believed that any secret service was inefficient by definition, simply because it was not subject to public scrutiny. An Anglo-American alliance would be even more a shambles than a one-nation operation. Then he'd no more time for speculation. His retreat from Rookwood had to be planned. So he looked through the used-car ads in the local paper until he found the one he wanted.

As he heard Laurence Adam approach, Middlemass lifted a book.

"Ah," Adam said. "Reading, eh? Something on wildlife, I expect?" Middlemass smiled and nodded since the book on his lap was called *Birds of the World* and that book was a foot wide and eighteen inches tall.

"How was Tolchester?" the squire of Rookwood asked.

"I didn't make it. Car trouble. Did you have a good day?"

"Can't say I did." Adam looked thwarted as he often did. He was a man of iron whim who inclined to sulk when his will was not obeyed. "Nothing but rabbits. The creatures stand still when one approaches, you know. It's almost like shooting farmyard hens."

Middlemass wanted to humour him for the moment. "And the rabbits are very grey, aren't they?" He meant that the rabbits of Rookwood had abandoned their burrows where the plague fleas lived and made their homes under bushes. Although they were now as grey as rabbits in hutches, they were still getting sick.

"Don't follow you," Adam said, "rabbits are always grey." He seemed to be staring at Middlemass's arm in the short-sleeved shirt. "I've seen some well-developed right arms," Adam said, "on tennis pros and so on. But yours is quite exceptional. Much larger muscle than your left. How did you develop it?"

"Chopping wood on my place in Vermont," Middlemass said and he lied. "Tell you who I think's well developed. Your gamekeeper."

"So he ought to be, out all day with a gun. Talking of shoots, there's something which might interest you on Friday. An otter hunt."

"An otter what?"

"No need to be alarmed, otters kill salmon, you know. A big meeting down at Milton St. Mary."

"You mean they kill *otters*?"

"Humanely. I shan't be there myself but you might find it interesting."

"I might. Why aren't you going?"

Adam walked across to the sideboard. "Some of these students, you know the people I mean, wasting their time and ours on government grants. They intend to try to break up the meeting. From my point of view, it could be embarrassing, but you're a stranger, after all. Would you like something to drink?"

"No, thanks, I'm thinking of making it an early night. In

the morning, I was wondering if . . ." He broke off, apparently embarrassed.

"In the morning? Whatever you want. Treat this place as your own."

"Well, I was wondering if I could take some pictures of the wildlife over the highway." Adam's pleasure was too obvious and Middlemass wondered who had recruited such a fool.

"Pictures, eh? The sparrow hawks and so on? Chap like you, a few photographs, a few remarks in the right quarters. Lending your weight, helping us preserve our wildlife. We're all keen conservationists, you know so long as things don't get out of hand."

Middlemass nodded, thinking of the gamekeeper and the slaughterhouse of a wood down below.

"Sorry I can't come myself," Adam said. "I'm driving to London tonight, as it happens. Staying at my club. Board meeting first thing tomorrow. Frightful bore."

Middlemass nodded again in sympathy. This was a very sudden departure, Adam was anxious to be out of the way. "Pity you can't come," Middlemass said. "But I've agreed to take Max Lawson, young man here on vacation. Four people would be too many, don't you think?"

"Four? Shona going, is she?" Adam asked.

"Well, no. She doesn't like the woods. Sometimes wonder why she came at all." Adam would take his chauffeur; the housekeeper and the helps lived out and the gardener's cottage was conveniently far away.

"Four people, did you say?"

"Well, I imagine the hawks are pretty cautious, aren't they? They have to be," Middlemass said. "They're moving on to the hghways to get away from . . . sportsmen. Is it true that English foxes are shifting into towns to dodge the huntsmen?"

177

"Are they? Damn them. I didn't know that. Our hunt has had a thoroughly rotten year. Who are you proposing to take besides Lawson?"

Middlemass accepted a port and praised it, "I was hoping to take your gamekeeper with me," he said. "If you can spare him. He really knows the woods, doesn't he?"

"He does indeed and I'm sure he'll be delighted." He telephoned the gamekeeper on the tapped line and gave instructions. "Just as I thought," Adam said as he replaced the receiver, "he's looking forward to it. A stalk will suit him admirably. A stalk with a camera, I mean."

22

THE LITTLE OWL in the wych elm gave its startling imitation of human laughter, the sound that has passed for ghostly mockery down the centuries. But Max had more on his mind than little owls or ghosts as he tried to tidy the shambles of his bedroom and hoped that the job would help him clear the clutter of his mind. Barney, Radford's dog, was not exactly helpful. As Max threw the last blanket over his bed, the dog caught the ends and pulled the bedclothes off again. When he gave up tidying and roamed restlessly, Barney padded behind him, beating out the time with his tail. Colonel Radford's retriever was an exception to an old rule. He had nothing in common with his master and Max sometimes wondered whether Radford had simply borrowed the dog for the job to add a touch of authenticity to the picture of the retired Army chaplain. The retriever would apparently accept any man as a friend. It might even wag its tail at Wainright.

Thinking about Wainright didn't help either, the Sky Eater had seemed too ready to accept Max's tale that they had spent hours in a garage having the Ford fixed.

But he had no worry about Wainright's gullibility or guile, he had to concentrate on the second part of the job—to "neutralise" Radford just before the sparrow hawk lark began. Radford had not come home, he had been missing through the night and now the dawn and the time to start for the motorway was all too close.

Max went downstairs to make coffee with the dog at his heels. When the kettle boiled, the dog was pulling at his trouser leg and he was forced to play with it, puppy play in the early hours of the morning.

He took the coffee into the living room, put the reassembled Sterling Paget under the couch cushions, then sat down on it. Even the gun was giving trouble. When Max put it together again, he had not been able to make the single shot position hold, and it would need the touch of a violinist on the trigger to keep the gun from burning ammunition. That nasty little hunk of metal vomited rounds, and it would be all too easy to empty it with the first burst, which had to register because it might also be the last. Why the hell hadn't he smuggled his familiar nine-millimetre Browning into England when he'd had the chance? Thanks to Hippo, he hadn't even had to stop at customs when he landed at Gatwick. Almost anything would have been more useful on this job than this dodgy Sterling Paget, even one of those ladies' handbag guns that the SAS sometimes carried, having seen too many spy films.

Barney sat on him, spilling the coffee and his thoughts, reminding him that the dog had to be considered in his plans. He had never known a sunnier retriever. But it had never been taught to keep its mouth soft, it stood a good twenty-six inches at the haunch and it had a neck muscle like a fighting bull. Supposing it *was* Radford's dog? It might change its ways if anything happened to its master. No dog was rougher than a retriever too sorely provoked.

Beyond that, the dog was almost totally silent. It might have been taken from its litter too early for it didn't bark except when it was chasing a ball. It certainly never barked or snarled when it was frightened or unhappy, only when it was dreaming. The dog had the long legs and the speed of which the Kennel Club disapproved. Max suspected some other strain had been introduced into what was officially a crossbred retriever. The colour was useful, the red-brown body for camouflage and the amber eyes to scare the hell out of someone who saw this silent dog and didn't know it. Max had seen Radford use this, ordering Barney to freeze to scare off a beggar.

If the first part of the operation went smoothly, Barney would be an excellent ally on the sparrow hawk guest. So Max play-wrestled with the dog, ordered it to freeze a few times, then led it to the garden shed that had once held the submachine gun. He took along Barney's basket, its favourite blanket, its wooly teddy bear and its headless doll. As he stroked the dog and whispered in its ear, Max realised how well equipped he was to be an airborne soldier. He was every inch the ruthless desperado. . . .

He heard the Daimler's engine but the car stopped some distance from the house. Max locked the garden shed, moved to the living room, lay down on the couch and put out the light. Radford would come through the garden gate, a long way from the shed. If Barney gave his usual greeting, a squeak like a shrew, Radford wouldn't hear. The dog hadn't even learned to bark to draw attention to itself, it would stand for an hour at the door, squeaking for someone to open up. . . .

Max could hear Radford taking off his shoes at the front door. He let the colonel pass through the hall and into the living room before he switched on the lamp and sat up, rubbing his eyes.

"Why aren't you upstairs in your own bed?" Radford

181

asked. The tall, bald man was playing the parish priest but he wasn't doing too well, his voice would have sounded more in keeping at a black mass.

"I couldn't sleep, Padre. I was worried about you. Scared something might have happened to your car."

Radford recomposed himself, then nodded severely, the Anglican priest listening to a confession. "Kind of you, but there was no need to worry." He was straightening chairs and lamps, the obsessional neurotic at full stretch, despite the measured voice and walk. But he stopped as he got nearer the couch. "What *is* that on the sofa by the by?"

"Coffee, sir. I'm afraid I spilled some. . . ."

"I'm not talking about coffee. You're always spilling coffee. I'm talking about Barney's hairs. That dog is not allowed on the sofa." Radford opened the kitchen door. "Barney, come here." Radford looked round the kitchen. "Where's the dog?" he asked. "And where's his box and his blanket?"

His back was turned and Max brought out the Sterling Paget. Question time was over. "Hands on your head," he said. "Now don't be silly, Colonel sahib. Put your hands on your head and do it slowly. It's your gun. You know it's performance."

"You wouldn't kill me," Radford said.

"I wouldn't bet on that. I'm not a bloody Frightener, Radford, but *you* were going to kill *me*. Thank you. Now get down on the floor. Slowly. Lie on your back. Spread your feet and hands."

He switched the light on and off, five times, then Todd strolled in. As he looked down at the colonel, Todd rubbed his supper from the corners of his mouth and began to grin.

"Colonel Padre Radford, Sergeant Todd," Max said formally. "No, he's not dead, Padre. You won't need your Common Prayer Book, just yet."

"Good morning, sir" Todd said. He came smartly to attention, marched forward as right marker and brought his left boot down on the Colonel's chest. Then he saluted slowly and obscenely with one finger.

"Everything else all right?" Max asked.

"Perfect," Todd said. "So many bastards sleeping out, it's like a meat beat jamboree. Wainright's in his nylon wanking pit and in his Mini, just short of Rookwood House. Prick Nose Prentice is in the laurels, maybe four hundred yards from the motorway. He's going to have a hard lie is Prick Nose. I never fancy sleeping with laurel up my crutch."

"He's got the set?"

"Bound to, inhe?" Todd said. "Let's deal with Holy Henry now." He took his boot from the colonel's chest and knelt beside him. First he stroked the bald head gently, then he let his hands settle round Radford's neck. "I think the padre wants to talk, sir," Todd said as Radford's eyes popped. "Permission for the colonel to speak, sir?" Max nodded and Todd relaxed his grip. "Permission granted, Jesus. But no fucking miracles. And whisper."

Radford fought for breath. "You must be mad, both of you," he said. "I don't know who this hooligan is but . . ."

"Oh, yes, you bloody do. Last time I saw you was back in Aden, just before two of them Airab politicians got it in the back. Didn't have a gun between them. Just about your weight, weren't they? How many machine-gunners did you need?"

"You know him?" Max asked.

"Yeah. But he was a civvy back in those days. Padre? Arseholes. Colonel Radford? Knickers."

"He's not even a priest?"

"Prick Nose will get his issue harp and wings before his civvy twat."

"Radford's not in the Army?" Max realised that the phoney chaplain routine was the safest one for a civilian among soldiers. Chaplains weren't supposed to know too much about the Army.

"Not even in the Band of Hope. He's a civvy secret service berk. Backroom boy. Knocks off people with his pen. Writes in other bastards' blood. Don't you, Charlie chaplain?"

"Who *is* this lunatic? Radford asked Max. "To think I showed you friendship. A roof over your head."

"Well, it's fell in," Todd said. "Where you been all night? Playing strip poker with the nuns again?"

Max nudged his sergeant. "Cut the patter, leave it to me. Where were you, Radford?"

"I don't intend to tell you. Wait until the police . . ." Todd clumped him and Radford's lip set firmly.

"No point in keeping him if he won't talk," Max said and Todd rammed the Sterling Paget's muzzle in Radford's ear. But he stayed silent and the time was passing.

"He'll talk," Todd said. "All he needs's a reminder." He took the muzzle from Radford's ear. "Where'll I give it to him? In the legs? Or hands, maybe? How about a splatter of the old stigmata?"

Radford refused to show fear and it was all too clear to Max that Todd was enjoying himself. "Give me the gun," he said. "Now tie him up." As Todd finished, Radford's head fell forward.

"Oh, for fuck's sake, he's fainted," Todd said. As he drew his knife, and prepared to prick Radford, Max knocked his hand away. He wasn't fooled by the fainting fit but he knew that Radford would hold out for a while and he didn't intend to satisfy Todd's blood lust.

"Might as well do him with the knife," Todd said, "save the ammunition, like."

Max pointed to the kitchen and Todd followed him. "Keep him for Middlemass" Max said. "His nerve'll crack but not right now. Let's turn this place over." They wrecked the locks on the drawers and found some interesting items including a code book, a heavily marked map of Rookwood, a better rope and enough ammunition to keep the Sterling Paget in business for some time.

"We still got a few minutes," Todd said. "I don't believe that bastard could be out this long. Let me carve him up a little. All I wanta do is write *Todd loves Radford* on him."

"No."

"He'll tell us his life story," Todd said. "From the first time he played with his mutton until his fingers fell off and the hair started sprouting on his palms."

"I said *no*. Use the second rope."

"Couldn't we do something different?" Todd asked. While he talked, he was busily tying up Radford with the powerful nylon rope which the ever-thoughtful chaplain had provided.

"Why?"

"He's the kinda creep who enjoys it. Supposing he gets a wet dream?" Radford's eyes flickered.

"Yeah, that brought you outa your trance, dinnen it?" Todd asked. "Now start talking." Radford became inert again.

"Let's go," Max said. "No time. It's nearly light."

They carried the bound Radford to his Daimler and locked him in the trunk. The considerate manufacturers had luckily provided an air vent, so that their kidnapped owner drivers would not suffocate. As Max leaned over Radford to fold him into place, the colonel padre spat in his eye. "Oh, dear me," Max said, "want a very un-Christian thing to do. I'll report you to the Chaplain General, so I will." He slammed the trunk then Todd drove the Daimler away.

185

23

IT WAS QUIET in the early morning at Rookwood House. The first of the helicopters passed overhead on its way to play war games over Salisbury Plain. Then a cock crowed as a light went on in a bedroom window. When the curlews were warning that dawn was near, Middlemass opened Shona's door quietly and stood there looking down at her. How could any girl who had spent all those years in the cross fire between Middlemass and his wife look so peaceful? He woke her by blowing on her hair. "Stop it, Max," she said, with her eyes still closed.

"Who?"

She opened her eyes. "Nobody. I was dreaming."

"I know that but how did you manage to look so pure?"

"Practice," she said, coming to swiftly and focusing on his clothes. "When do you start yodelling?" she asked as she looked at the German hunting cap and coat.

"I don't yodel. That was Johnny Weismuller, my *elder* brother," he said.

"I thought you'd given your Goering costume away?"

"I'll do that one day. If you'll get up *now*." He'd kept the hunting coat and cap ever since he had taken it from its dead owner. In his adult life, he'd killed nothing except men but the warm and waterproof coat was suited to the woods and the game pocket would hide the bulk of the .358 magnum he'd taken from the agent in his New York apartment. Besides it appealed to what Doctor Gellner called his sense of black farce to wear the shooting clothes of a nation that had once hunted him so hard.

"I'm getting up, Dad. How about getting out?"

"Sure you can drive the horse box, Shona?"

"If I can drive your Ford Frightener, I can drive anything."

"Let's go over it one more time."

"Do we have to, Dad?"

"Yes. Unless you're certain you've got total recall?" He was talking gently to her, taking the sting out of the words and he waited until she was completely awake. "You drive the horse box into a rest area near Tolchester . . . no one's going to imagine a horse box has been abandoned. Then you catch the bus into town. Where do you get off?"

"By the town hall, Dad."

"That's it. And you'll find the used-car dealer's lot is just behind that. What's your story there?"

"I want something very cheap and very roomy to take a gang of kids camping."

"And . . ."

"I let him know that I'm willing to pay cash on the line."

"Fine, but don't rush it. Let him try to sell you a beat up station wagon and so on until you suddenly notice the ambulance. It will probably be at the back, among the junk."

"And I think this light ambulance is the greatest, the most British thing. I really *want* it and I'm going to give it a pop art coat of paint. So I buy it."

"No, you don't. You haggle, Shona. Americans in England are bargainers these days. Don't make him suspicious. You give him fifty pounds less than he asks for the first time around."

"Suppose he's honest, Dad? Suppose he wants the hospital's name painted out before the ambulance leaves the yard?"

"No used-car dealer's that honest. Tell him you can't live without that ambulance. You'll bring it back and show it to him once it's painted with stripes and flowers. If he doesn't have the log book and the other documents, you'll pick them up later. Now the route . . ."

"I've memorised that. Don't talk about it, huh? You'll confuse me."

"You're not confused now?"

"Over what, Dad?"

"Max Lawson."

"If you don't get out, Dad, I'll never get dressed."

He kissed her on the brow and walked out. At least she was safe, fairly safe, the only one who was.

As he left the house the light was strengthening and he savoured the sights and sounds and smells, despite the instant ulcer in his stomach. Shona and Gellner and others believed that he enjoyed being hunted for the hell of it. But they were wrong, although he'd never tried to correct them. He knew when the odds against were too high, as they were this morning. But he had to have the radio set, he had to deal with the local opposition and he knew no other way.

For all his tension, he stopped to watch an albino dunnock, a rare sight, it looked like a sparrow that had been through a spin dryer. Then the keeper joined him in the drive.

"It'll be fair light soon," the keeper said as he touched his hat. "And good weather by the look of things."

"Fine. I certainly appreciate you coming with me." Middlemass felt sorry for the keeper; maybe it wasn't his fault he was such a creep, a walking cringe of obsequiousness. Maybe people like Laurence Adam were responsible for that. But it hadn't been Adam who had given the keeper those sly eyes. No one had forced him to become the butcher of the local wildlife. Middlemass drove his sympathy out as his purpose hardened. "Chilly still, isn't it?" he asked.

24

Max was wandering up the track when Wainright made his usual demon king appearance from behind a tree. "You're late," he said.

"Sorry, sir," Max said. "It's my Deputy Dawg alarm clock. It keeps on letting me down. I'd buy a new one, but I'm stuck for half a book of Green Shield stamps."

Wainright's lip twitched but he was gazing at Barney, who was sniffing at his boots. "What the hell are you doing with Colonel Radford's dog?"

"What was I supposed to do with the beast?" Max asked. "Colonel Radford hasn't been back all night."

"No time for your puerile jokes," Wainright said. The Sky Eater hadn't shaved or stood near enough to a bar of soap or even given his beautiful hair its two hundred brush strokes. "Why the dog?"

"It followed me," Max said. "Colonel Radford's been out all night. He's never shown. I heard his Daimler then it drove away again."

For once Wainright was looking at him directly instead of into the invisible mirror perched before his face. "Let's go back and check on that story."

"Why not?" The dog was still sniffing at Wainright's boots.

The Sky Eater almost kicked it, caught Max's expression then changed his mind.

"You're telling me that Colonel Radford hasn't briefed you?" Wainright asked.

"Come and see for yourself. Off, Barney. We're going home."

"Stay where you are," Wainright said.

"All right. But what would Radford brief me on?" Max asked. "The First Corinthians?"

Wainright produced a battery razor and began to shave. The batteries were weak, the razor tugged and Max enjoyed the whole performance. "I've done what I was told," he said. "I've bet Middlemass there are hawks above the motorway. We're going to look, just like you told me, check? And the dog makes it even cosier. So what was Radford going to brief me on again?"

Wainright put the razor away before the shave was finished. "I'd love to have you in a plane, Lawson."

"More than I can say for you, *sir*. I'd have to pack my parachute myself. And I'd want you jumping ahead of me. What were you going to say about Colonel Radford?"

Wainright appeared to be practising Yoga breathing to retain control while he looked at Max's duffle coat, dyed a vivid blue. "Where did you get that ridiculous garment?"

"My Cruel Sea, you mean? From a Red Cross shop," Max said. "Very warm. Cost me a quid, worth every penny. Come to that, what are you doing wearing a red sweater, sir? Have the local hawks gone colour blind?"

Wainright raised his hand so swiftly that Max hoped he would try to hit him. Instead the Sky Eater rubbed the back of his neck to ease the tension.

"When did you last see Colonel Radford?"

"Breakfast yesterday," Max said, "and he forgot to say grace, again."

"Very well, your orders are simple. You'll take Mr. Middlemass towards the gap in the silver birches by the motorway." He gave the map reference and Max nodded.

"You'll let him go to the edge of the motorway alone."

"That's for sure," Max said. "I don't want to be there when he sees nothing. Sparrow hawks, for Christ's sake. We've more chance of seeing a bloody albatross with all those helicopters buggering about."

"There are hawks on that stretch of motorway," Wainright said. "He will see one or some similar bird."

"Sorry, Saint Francis," Max said, "I didn't recognise you in red."

"You'll stop just short of the motorway, Lawson. You'll see a helicopter travelling on a north and south flight path. As it passes overhead, you'll point out to Mr. Middlemass that a hawk is just above the motorway."

"Supposing it isn't?"

"Point to some other bird," Wainright said.

"I've got it," Max said, "I'll point out the mocking bird in the wursle tree. Or the condor crapping on the overpass." He was giving up hope that the Sky Eater's temper would snap.

"When the helicopter approaches for a second time, point to Middlemass and then get down."

"Why?" Max asked.

"The purpose of this exercise is to draw out Middlemass' enemies," Wainright said. "I've let it be known that he'll be walking near the motorway this morning. We think the enemy will reconnoitre."

"The Arabs, you mean?"

"The enemy, Lawson."

"Supposing they do more than reccy?" Max asked. "How come I'm unarmed?"

"Good question," Wainright said. "But we're certain they won't attack just yet. If we flush them out now, they won't live to try. The helicopter pilot will be looking for them as his main task. It is also essential that he should know Middlemass for later protection. You understand?"

"Think so," Max said. He understood all too well, but he wanted more details. "But wouldn't it be better if you had a signal contact with the chopper?"

"We'll point, that's enough," Wainright said. "The pilot will recognise my red sweater and your blue coat. But he must be certain of Middlemass for future reference. Understood?" His story was threadbare, for how was the helicopter to know that Max was wearing blue, without future wireless contact?

"Why should I get down on my own?" Max asked. "Wouldn't it be better if Middlemass got down as well?"

"We want him in front. Once the pilot is satisfied that he'll recognise him again, he'll search thoroughly for the enemy."

"I think I follow," Max said. Without Radford to guide him, the Sky Eater wasn't exactly a spellbinding storyteller.

"Right, move. And get rid of that dog."

"Why? He's bombproof," Max said, knowing that he'd no more to gain by delay.

"He's what?"

"Bombproof," Max spoke loudly, for the second time. "It takes a helluva lot to frighten him. Not even you could . . ."

Wainright turned swiftly but not fast enough and Todd clumped him with the heavy hammer from Radford's impressive range of household tools.

"Why the hell did you take so long?" Max said.

"Sorry, I got interested," Todd said. "Bloody hell, a helicopter and a motorway. That old gag. That's what's wrong with Frighteners nowadays. No initiative, no real pride in their work." He thumped Wainright again to make sure he'd be cooperative, then stripped off the red sweater and began to bind him. "Better shift, sir," Todd said. He handed over the sweater and the hammer.

When Max joined Middlemass and the keeper, they had reached the scruffy clump of thuya trees that were fighting for survival against the rabbits, the weeds and the chalk in the soil. The keeper touched his hat to greet Max but his cold dark eyes, his snake eyes, were on the dog.

"Morning," Middlemass said. "Brought your camera?"

"Yes," Max said, "and it's loaded."

"Good-looking dog," Middlemass said. "Where did you get it?"

"Borrowed it for this jaunt," Max said. "The owner won't be needing him today."

They walked with the keeper for a bit, then let him walk ahead. As he went, his gum boots squelched as he brought his heels down and his head lolled from side to side. It was a clumsy but fast and confident stride, the keeper was reminding the woods that he was master there, under God and Laurence Adam.

Middlemass dropped on one knee and loaded his camera, his fingers working on the camera while Max briefed him. "How do you read it?"

"I don't like it. It's too obvious," Max said, "there has to be another catch."

"Maybe, but we have to play it out," Middlemass said.

"We're going ahead as planned?"

"As planned. Start limping now. Why did you bring that dog?"

"Because it would sniff out a Frightener in a sewage

195

plant," Max said as he began to limp. Middlemass stuffed the Sky Eater's red sweater into his deep pocket and caught up with the keeper as he crossed the ridge.

As they passed, the pheasants ran to meet them, greeting the keeper who hand-fed and nursed them, then arranged for them to be massacred, mainly by grisly old men who knew that their own deaths were at hand. They passed jays hanging by their claws. A dead badger was on display and squirrels slaughtered by the score, all hung up to show the squire that the keeper had real enthusiasm for his work.

"I think Mister Lawson's got something in his shoe," Middlemass said, "but he'll catch up if we take it easy."

The keeper simply nodded and began to walk faster, increasing the distance between him and Lawson with his dog. As Middlemass had expected, the keeper wanted to keep away from the man who'd wrecked his badger snares and from any large silent dog; he would be afraid of a dog he hadn't personally cowed.

As he turned, Middlemass saw Max on the far side of the ridge with the dog trotting so close to him that its leash was slack. The dog had a jaunty stride, a rippling back and a steady tail wag. It looked as if it had been born in sunshine with its red-gold colouring and its amber eyes. Middlemass hoped that nothing would happen to the man or the retriever and he also hoped he was more worried about Lawson than the dog.

Max let him cross the ridge before he walked toward the laurels where Prentice was hiding. By now, the trooper should have signalled to the helicopter pilot that Max was wearing blue and that Middlemass up ahead had a green hunting coat and hat. But to make quite sure, Max let Barney examine a rabbit hole, then sniff around for shrews before he guided him toward the laurel clump. He wasn't particularly frightened and he recognised the symptoms all too well. Max had died of his imagination on many a sleepless night, but fear seemed to desert him when it was needed. At the moment of impact his defence mechanism was usually faulty. . . .

Barney was straining at the lead. The dog was silent as ever but his mouth was dripping saliva and his tail was feathering. Barney stopped and pointed, one foreleg extended with the paw elegantly slack, the nose and tail in line, the body absolutely still. Poor bloody animal, he was anxious to make friends with Prick Nose Prentice, of all people. Barney dropped his stance, looked up at Max, then wagged his tail. Max couldn't see that dog living to any age.

"Prentice? You there?" Max was whispering. He could hear nothing but the dog pointed again, looked up at Max in frustration, then began to drag on his lead. "Prentice? I've got to talk to you." He thought that Todd and even the dog had been wrong until he heard a laurel twig snap. Laurel always looked like excellent cover but Prentice didn't seem to know how noisy it could be.

"Prentice, I've got new orders for you." He waited. "From Major Wainright." He waited again. "Prentice, are you coming out or am I coming in?"

In the long silence, he began to wonder if Todd was around. He led Barney round in a circle, the dog's nose twitched, he seemed to be confused, then he settled for sniffing at Prentice again. There was no proof that Todd was near enough but there was clear evidence that Prentice was highly suspicious. If his suspicion deepened and Todd still didn't show, Max would be the first to go and his mind cleared wonderfully. He knew now that he would kill rather than be killed. It didn't look as if he'd be given the choice, but he had nothing to gain by changing the plan now.

"Prentice, come out of there or I'll pee on you, you bloody bush." How the hell had he ever got himself into this situation? "Prentice, I don't intend to shout. You want me to come in there and drag you out?"

Barney was enjoying the game, straining still, dragging Max toward the laurel. As he tightened his grip on the lead, he heard Prentice cock his machine gun and he wished that he believed in something. Prentice was crawling forward so quietly that Max had to follow Barney's nose to be certain the trooper was moving. If he kept this up in dense undergrowth, he'd be a difficult target for Todd, assuming the sergeant was around. If he was, Barney did not know about it.

"That your idea of fieldcraft, Prentice?" Max asked. "Don't make so much bloody noise. Get off your fucking knees. What you think you are? A python with piles?" Barney showed him that Prentice was nearer and still crawling. "Get up, Prick Nose."

At this final insult, Prentice rose and took murderous aim. Max had expected his last thoughts on earth would be profound but he was aware of nothing beyond the Sterling Paget pointed at him. They'd guessed the trooper would be armed with a noisy Japanese .223 machine gun or a Colt Commander. But Prentice had another Sterling Paget. He could kill Max without Middlemass ever hearing, kill without making more noise than the crack of a falling branch. . . .

Prentice's aim wavered. He was disconcerted by the wholly unconcerned dog examining his boots. Max didn't even know he'd dropped the lead.

Todd fired over Max's shoulder. The single-shot control on Radford's Sterling Paget failed to hold and the gun fired a burst. Prentice's face broke up before he fell then the shots drove his body along the ground.

"Wouldn't want to have to dress him for the funeral,"

Todd said. "Some poor sod would have to use a lotta glue."

Max grabbed Barney's lead as the dog heaved away. Barney was terrified and Max was so badly shaken that he had hardly the strength to hold the dog. "Get him a sledge and an Eskimo," Todd said, "and get me a better gun next time. What a bloody waste of slugs."

Max sat down before his legs folded. Why hadn't he thought this out? The only way for Todd was to follow *them*, not Prentice, staying upwind of the dog and letting Max muffle the approach. The simplest rules of fieldcraft had deserted him with their normal stealth. Why the hell had he expected Todd to come from behind the trooper, the way they did in cowboy films?

"Glad you made it," Max said as he tied the trembling dog to a bush.

"Fucking grateful, aren't you? What chance did you have if I hadn't showed?" Todd asked as he recovered the radio set. It was switched off, at least the helicopter pilot and the others on the wavelength couldn't have heard the machine gun.

"Thanks."

"That all you gotta say? You wish it was you I had to cover up with bloody branches?" Prentice's hands were tightening on the Sterling Paget but Todd extracted the submachine gun, cleaned it, then wiped his hands fastidiously on the ferns. "Sticky, innit? Sweaty bastard, Prentice, always was."

Max was pulling up ground elder by the root. "Can't you hear me, Mr. Lawson? I'm running outta jokes to cheer you up. You reckon this another filthy murder by dirty bastard Todd? Him or you? Which had to be the one?"

Max dug up a second root. "You've got it wrong," he said. "Why did you take so bloody long? He nearly did me, Fuckface." He realised he was talking like Todd without conscious effort. He was also thinking like Todd and caring almost as

199

little as Todd about the death of Trooper Prentice. It wouldn't take long now. He'd only have to live for a few more days, then he could sign off as an emotional cripple.

"How do you mean? Hadta get into position, dinnen I?"

"You must have been in position when he was crawling," Max said.

Todd looked incredulous. "You think I shoulda scatter-gunned the shrubbery and risked writing off that radio?"

Max took the point, the radio set was more important than his life. "Thanks," he said, "I'll do the same for you one day."

"Some hope. Two targets like that in one lifetime? I was so bloody close I coulda pissed on him if I'd got the right trajectory. How about getting outta your Rule Brittania shit order?" Max took off the naval duffle coat, then Todd strapped the radio and the other Sterling Paget to his back. "You screwed up the single shots on that one, so you can have it," the sergeant said. "How about it, though? Two silent shooters on one day. We gotta be the best armed berks in the whole of Sherwood Forest."

Todd stood back and admired his handiwork when Max put on the duffle coat again. "You'll have to walk stiff," he said, "like you was having impure thoughts about Miss Middlemass." He laughed at Max's expression but he stayed out of fist range. "Thought as much," Todd said. "You're a right sucker for the woman, aren't you? You like a bit of moonlight and roses before you dip your wick. Best of luck, though. I'd be after her myself if I stood any bloody chance." He held out his hand. "Sorry," he said. "I didn't mean no offence, no aggravation, right?"

"No," Max said, but he did not take Todd's hand.

"Sorry I got no smelling salts, sir."

"I'm all right," Max said. The disturbing thing was he was

telling the truth. He had been too close to death to care about Prentice. He felt no more about the trooper than he would have done about a well-squashed wasp. "I'll be okay."

"Not *you*. It's your dog that's got the vapours. That was all we needed on this lark. An anteye-blood-sports hound."

25

ON THE FAR SIDE of the ridge, Middlemass heard the machine gun. He had expected single shots or a short burst but this sounded as if Todd and Prentice were fighting it out. He'd listened for a sound like the crack of a beech branch that had lost its interest in life, but this noise suggested the earth flail of a heavy limb dragged from an ancient elm. If Todd had fought and lost, he would know all too soon. . . .

The gamekeeper was also listening. "What was that?" Middlemass asked.

"Tree of some kind," the keeper said. "Some of the foresters round here don't know their job, look. So long as it don't trouble my pheasants, it's no worry o' mine."

"Or mine," Middlemass said. "I think I'd better wait for Mr. Lawson, though. He's having trouble with his foot or his dog. Or maybe he's gotten lost. Go ahead and I'll catch up."

"Shouldn't wonder it's that dog." The keeper's smile was at once ingratiating and conspiratorial. "A queer creature that, bit of everything, a Hampshire hound." He touched his hat and moved on before Middlemass saw the helicopter. It was flying as high and sedately as the conventional Royal Air

Force choppers. But it was not on their normal flight path. This machine was not heading for Wiltshire, it was flying toward the highway.

Middlemass made sure the pilot could see him as the machine flew over. He watched until the helicopter was almost out of sight, then it began to grow larger again. The pilot had turned, he was coming back for his second run.

When he saw the blue of Max's duffle coat on the ridge, Middlemass was reassured. He dropped into the cover of a rhododendron that was past its best, the holes in the foliage like gunports. From there he could keep an eye out for the helicopter, make sure the keeper was on the right course and wait for Max. . . .

Barney charged into the bush and licked him as if they had been lifelong friends. "Prentice?" Middlemass asked.

"You can forget him. I've got the set."

"Fine, now let the pilot see us."

They cleared the bush and began to walk toward the gap as the helicopter passed overhead, travelling parallel with the road as the Air Force choppers usually travelled.

"He won't be long," Middlemass said. "He'll make another sweep then come in for his final run. Maybe he's puzzled by wireless silence but . . ."

"He won't be," Max said, "that's standard practice. No news is good news."

"Even better. I'm following the keeper to the gap. Keep to my right and don't let the keeper know how close you are."

Just short of the gap where the gamekeeper was waiting the soil became sour and the cover was thick with rhododendrons and ferns and birch trees ruling all the way to the road. Once they were in that temperate jungle, the pilot would have no hope of seeing them.

"Young Lawson. He's dragging his feet," Middlemass said.

204

"He's not so sure we'll see anything to write home about. How do you figure our chances?"

The keeper did not meet his eyes. "Well, sir . . . this road's off my beat, like."

"You don't expect to see anything, either?"

"Now, I didn't say that, sir. If the squire says they vermin . . . the hawks and such be there, they'll be there, like enough. Not every day but sometimes, if you take my meaning."

"I take your meaning." Middlemass kept well away from the gap. A double bluff could be operating and a marksman with a rifle might be covering that opening. But he had to look at the telegraph lines beyond the highway, to keep up appearances, so he climbed into a silver birch that commanded the road. Middlemass looked along the telegraph lines, then blinked. There *was* a sparrow hawk after all but it was clinging to the lines in a weird way. He focused his powerful binoculars then restrained the laugh. The hawk on the line was an excellent example of the taxidermist's art. The sparrow hawk was stuffed and tied in position. Studying it, he remembered a derisive American's crack that the British Special Air Service were the Sky Diving Majorettes.

Middlemass hid his binoculars, then scrambled down from the tree. "I gave up too easily," he said to the keeper, "there *is* a sparrow hawk. I want a picture of it with me in the foreground. You understand how this camera works?"

"I'm not rightly sure," the keeper said.

"Not difficult, let me show you." Middlemass made the operation of the camera look as complicated as a space laboratory.

"I'll have to go, I'll try it," the keeper said.

"Sorry, that isn't good enough. That bird won't hang around when it sees a human. I've got one chance. Can you use this camera or can't you?"

As the keeper hesitated, Middlemass could hear the heli-copter coming back. "Yes or no?" he asked.

"Now if it was a shotgun . . ."

"But it's not a shotgun. Hang on, I've got it. All you'll see of me is my back and my hat. The ferns will hide the rest. So you can wear my coat and hat and I can take the picture? Check?"

Before the keeper could argue, Middlemass pulled off his coat and hat. "Don't worry," he said, "I'll keep out of sight. I want you to go to that gap, get up slowly and point to the sparrow hawk. Got it?" The keeper nodded uncertainly as Middlemass stuck the deerstalker on his head and helped him into the hunting coat. "If you get up very slowly and stand stock still, the sparrow hawk won't bother about you. Right?" The keeper was slow with the coat until Middlemass pressed money on him. "I'll double that if we get the right pictures. I can't wait to show these shots to Lawson . . . and the folks back home."

While the gamekeeper crawled toward the gap, Middle-mass put on the Sky Eater's red sweater. The early morning traffic was now so close and so noisy that the keeper seemed unaware of the approaching helicopter. He froze behind a silver birth then he eased round the tree toward the gap so slowly that he hardly appeared to move. In the clear he stood motionless then his arm work was equally inspired—almost worthy of Marcel Marceau—as his right hand moved slowly upward until it pointed to the sparrow hawk.

Middlemass was puzzled by the helicopter. This had to be its main run, but it wasn't losing height or changing speed. He'd assumed that it meant to drive the victim into the high-way by dropping fast, turning beam on and blowing the man into the road with its fans. . . .

Middlemass rose in his red sweater and pointed to the

keeper, then dropped. On his right, Max rose in his blue
duffle coat then vanished again. As Middlemass rolled over on
his back, he understood.

A snatch basket swung from the chopper as it sailed se-
renely overhead, unnoticed by the traffic. The snatch basket
caught the keeper, lifted him off his feet then dropped him
on the road. Then the empty basket rose as the chopper
gained height.

The first car in the nearside lane missed the keeper with a
wild swerve that took it off the highway, over the verge and
into a copse of young fir trees. The car in the fast lane was
burning its brakes as it swung out and cannoned off the safety
barrier. The car in the centre lane was also braking desper-
ately but it struck the keeper with its nearside bumper and
pushed him back into the slow lane where the driver of the
articulated truck had no chance at all. From the sound, that
truck ran over the keeper with every outside pair of its double wheels.

Middlemass climbed back into the birch where he could
study the body. The man in his green hunting coat was
squashed like a frog.

They had meant to kill him all right, his blackmail was no
longer an indemnity. But for the moment at least, the world
could be persuaded that John Middlemass was dead.

26

THE EDGES OF THE TRACK were overgrown as the elders and the ash, the hazel and the thorn moved in to reclaim it. Overhead, their branches touched and formed a roof of trees, thatched with wild clematis, providing air cover against helicopters. As he dragged the dog, driven dizzy by the scents, Max conceded Middlemass' gift for ground.

At the end of the track the old black barn leaned, held together by bitumen and hope with its rotten door moving in a nonexistent wind. This was the signal he expected, the dog pulled him toward the door as it scented Shona.

As she closed the door and leaned on it, she looked as he felt, weak with relief. Max slipped the dog's leash before it dragged him against her, into the contact they were both avoiding. Then they looked at each other until it was difficult to bridge the gap with speech.

"Dad? Todd? Everything all right?"

"I think so," he said.

"You don't want to talk about it?"

"Not a lot." He saw Prentice's face as it broke up. He saw the gamekeeper standing like a war memorial just before the snatch basket caught him. Max could still hear the motorway battle of bumpers, brakes and horns. He was not yet covered with the cold and callous skin of killers, after all, but he felt no need to congratulate himself. His involvement with casual victims on the motorway was minor stuff, manslaughter at worst. He had already become an accessory to three murders, twice on that morning alone. For the first time he understood that a guilty man might shift his burden as he held up his wrists for the handcuffs. But he did not believe in God or the laws, so he could neither confess to a priest or a policeman.

"You don't have to talk about it," she said.

"I don't want to start talking in case I can't stop." Prentice was still haunting him. His face kept breaking up.

"You frightened?"

"Rigid," Max said.

"I'll bet you've learned how to deal with it though," she said. "Todd and you. You've been through it."

Once more he silently cursed Todd for his oblique boasting.

"I can sometimes read lips," Shona said. "One of the things my father taught me. Are you really scared?"

"You don't think I'd boast about it, do you?"

"But you've had things like this to be scared about before."

"Not like this," he said. He had a picture of a night in Arabia when he'd been almost paralyzed with fear before the action began, but that night had been one of the times by which a man remembers and measures his life. . . .

"Not quite like this but near enough?" Shona asked.

"No," Max said. "Last time I *knew* what I had to be frightened about. . . . You've read the Taoist stuff?" He wasn't certain whether he was more afraid of Middlemass and how he would act than he was of the entire SAS. "And Zen and so on?"

"Some."

"That bit. I thought I understood it once. The idea that hounding your own mind with your own mind is ridiculous. You start being afraid of fear and you go round in circles. With me?"

"Yes," she said. "Think so. If you don't clutch at your mind, the anxiety goes away."

"That's nearer," Max said. "Bloody hell I thought I'd got it. Every time I read it, I think I've got it, then it goes away again." A long, long time before Wittgenstein, these Chinese jokers had worked out that death was not a part of life. "The mind's supposed to have better things to work on. A tree for example. The way a chestnut tree starts sprouting in the spring. Or just standing here looking at you."

"That's nonsense," Shona said, "You're still hounding your mind, still driving it, telling it what to think."

"Maybe so," Max said. "Will you buy this then? This is one of the moments for me. It's like that night in Arabia. . . .

"What night in Arabia?"

"Never mind that night in Arabia. This is better. You believe me?"

"No," she said, "but it's a good try. Thanks for trying."

"Look at me and answer again," he said.

As she looked at him, the smile faded and she started rubbing at the corner of her mouth with her fingers. She was spreading makeup but she didn't seem to know or care.

"Do you believe me?" Max asked.

"I don't want to believe you," she said. "My life, your life, they're complicated enough."

"Supposing you let my mind float and try again."

"I won't let it float. Is that Radford's dog?"

"Don't worry about the dog. Try floating," Max said as Barney lost his interest in Shona. The dog walked judiciously round the light ambulance, appraising the remaining blank

211

spaces left for its signature. At last it signed, looked at Max to witness the deed, then drove a pigeon into the rafters.

"What do we *do* with the dog?" she asked.

"Leave that to the boss. He shouldn't be long." Middlemass had gone off to signal Zurich.

"Boss. My father's really gotten to you, hasn't he? You're not scared of him, are you?"

"Not physically," Max said.

"That's not what I mean."

"I know what you mean and I don't know how to answer." How could he tell her how he felt about her father? Could he say that he'd never met a monster before? Or that he couldn't define his feelings for him as admiration, awe, dread or even disbelief? Middlemass ordered men and took lives like a general without a general's detachment from the battle, or a general's total belief in himself and his rotten cause. . . .

"Whatever you feel, don't show it to him," Shona said.

"Why?"

"Dad, he plays a part and if other people buy his act he believes it himself."

"And if they don't buy it?"

"Well, he's like an actor without the lines. He doesn't really know who he is. He isn't all that certain that there's anybody home."

"You sure he's like that?"

"Certain. Because I'm a bit like that myself," she said.

Max was puzzled. "What's so unusual about that?" he asked. He felt the same about himself. Didn't everybody?

"I don't think they do," Shona said. "I think a lot of people have a pretty firm idea of what they think they are. And who's going to tell them if they're wrong?"

"You answered something I didn't ask," he said. He wasn't aware of drowning his guilt and his confusion. They seem to have dived on their own. "I thought it but I didn't say it. It's a helluva long time since anybody's been tuned in to me."

"Or me," she said.

"I mean this is ridiculous, isn't it?" He had a hammer and a submachine gun when he really needed a lute.

The silence lasted, then Shona said, "We could talk about the weather, but it isn't all that different from yesterday."

"Everything's different from yesterday," he said. "I wasn't certain yesterday. I thought maybe I was fooling myself. But I'm not. I've got in deep with you."

"What am I supposed to say to that?"

"Nothing, I'm just telling you about me."

"If you feel anything about me . . . well, that's wild. And you'll forget about it when things are normal."

"When do you think things will get normal?"

"What I'm trying to tell you is . . . don't let it show."

"You ashamed?" he asked. "You needn't be. I'm the one that's floating."

"What I'm trying to tell you is, don't let it show with Dad. He'll use it, he'll use you."

"He's going to do that anyway."

He was closing in again so she turned away and sat down on the barn floor. "There's maybe another way," she said. "He might see it differently if *I* was crazy about *you.*"

As he sat down beside her, the dog got in between them, a jealous chaperon.

"Let me in on the joke," she said.

"No joke. He wouldn't believe you, that's all."

"Why not?"

"Because he's not a fool. Because . . ." Max trailed off, aware that she was angry.

"Why wouldn't he believe me?" Shona asked. "Who told you it wasn't true?"

A Dream of Treason

"Nobody."

"You're sure I'd be lying?"

"Positive," he said.

"Maybe you can read me better than I can?"

Max was stunned by the late fall of fortune. Supposing this was on? Just supposing . . . he stopped supposing. He needed all this as much as he needed a hole in the head and a hole in the head was a distinct probability.

"You listening?" she asked.

"I'm trying not to," Max said. He'd flown so high that he hadn't looked down to see the cable stretching from him to the ground. She was offering to protect him, to get him out of this somehow.

"Thanks," she said, "thanks a lot."

"No, listen. I'm a lousy liar like you said, so I'll give the truth a whirl. I could tell you that I fancied you something rotten but it isn't as simple as that."

"Keep talking," she said.

"It's a bit like being up and away on speed or something. Don't get the wrong idea, will you? I gave up chemical kicks a long time ago."

"Me, too," she said. "I think it took me a year to get over a sip of acid. I didn't even have a bad trip. But maybe it was bad stuff."

"Funny. Same thing happened with me. Our lot. We find it as hard to talk about . . . love as my old man did about funerals or death. I think I love you but . . ."

"But?"

"But I thought that about somebody else and it wasn't too long ago. Out in Arabia."

"Pretty easy thing to happen in Arabia," she said.

"No, she was special. That's why I don't trust myself or what I feel about you. Except that . . . skip it."

214

"Except what?"

"Well, I thought I'd be carrying a torch for her, forever. But it got lower and lower after I saw you. Now it's snuffed, it's out. What does that make me?"

"Same as other people," she said. "It happened to me. And he was British, too."

"There you are, we're a couple of bleeding hearts born in the wrong age group. . . . hey, hang about. Who was this bloody Britisher? Who *was* he?" She started laughing.

"All right, okay," Max said. "What I'm trying to say is . . . I don't want any favours from the court. I don't want you to intercede and ask for a reprieve. I'm in this with . . . well, with Sweeney Todd and here I stick."

She was still laughing and the dog was as baffled as Max, it gave her quick, tentative licks to placate her.

"I must have missed something," Max said.

"You're here with Sweeney Todd and here you stick," she said. "That's fabulous. You can't make a speech about standing by me. So you're loyal to Todd, aren't you? Back to back."

"You want me to make a speech, Shona?"

"No."

"Fine, I'll make it. I love you and I'm not going anyplace without you. It's bloody ridiculous, but it's true. It doesn't make me happy, in fact it hurts but I love you. Will that do?"

"No," she said and then they heard the car. Before he checked the door, he knew from Barney that it was Radford's Daimler so he led the dog to the shed behind the barn and tied him up, out of sight and hearing. The dog did not whine at first, its look of reproach was enough.

Todd got out and helped him open the door. "How's your dandruff?" he asked.

"Not bad but my fowl pest's something terrible," Max said, relieved to rejoin the act, scared that what he felt for Shona would show. "Got the two boys interested in bondage?"

"Yeah and it's time we got Holy Henry out." Todd stopped to listen while the dog whimpered from the shed. "Mourning his master already. That piss-pot priest might go and die on us from bloody spite."

27

MIDDLEMASS SAT BRAIDING straws while the others watched him. Radford and the Sky Eater's first interrogation was over and they were strapped to the bunks in the ambulance. It was time to bury the Daimler beneath a small mountain of straw, then shift. But Middlemass went on braiding, while the dog whimpered in the outhouse.

"How about the dog?" Max asked.

"How about the humans?" Todd was always uneasy in the presence of a silent thinker. Shona lay on her back looking at the rafters, knowing that Middlemass wouldn't consciously hear them until he had made up his mind. She waited until he dropped the straw.

"What was the bad news from Zurich, Dad?"

"Yes," he said and she gave up trying, as he'd intended. Middlemass hadn't made contact with Zurich; it looked as if his man there had been taken. But the capture of Radford had almost made up for that. Colonel Radford had been so self-consciously clever that he'd given Middlemass invaluable help without even knowing it. Middlemass was now certain the British had tried to make an accidental killing look almost like a public execution to be blamed on the Americans. They wouldn't find it hard to persuade the Sultan of Doha

217

that the Americans had arranged for Middlemass's execution while the British attempted to guard him. It figured that the British would try to muscle in on Doha and snatch the oil from under American noses; that had always been in the cards. Now it was no longer enough for Middlemass to let the Sultan know he was still alive or that his letters had been intercepted and forgeries sent in their places. The Sultan needed something more, something that would rekindle his hatred of all Western powers. He had to be upset, he had to withdraw into his palace and brood. Middlemass wanted him to stay there, silent among his silenced slaves and his scent-drenched wives who wore Paris finery underneath their purdah; until he could get to Doha in person. . . .

"What are we going to make of my sudden death?" Middlemass asked and even Shona looked puzzled. "That object on the road was wearing my clothes, and it's going to take a good pathologist long enough to work out who or what he was. Nobody's going to miss the keeper for a while."

Max thought his mind had gone, his answer was gentle. "How about the Frighteners? They'll know." Prentice and his boys had been off the air too long, and neither Radford nor Wainright had reported back. "How long are we going to give them to seal us off?"

"Not long enough," Middlemass said. "So they'll know. Will they tell the police?"

"Not for a day or so," Max said, "but. . . ."

"A day or so's all we need," Middlemass said. "We've got to let the newspapers know I'm dead."

"Yeah. Maybe we'd better shift and talk about it later," Todd said.

"We tip off the newspapers that I'm dead," Middlemass said. "We let the story build high enough, then we turn up in a newspaper office two days from now. That's Saturday. So it has to be the Sunday *Times* or the *Observer* or the *Telegraph*."

"Meantime, we tip off one of the news agencies?" Max asked. He was beginning to get the drift. If the story could be printed fast enough, there was no chance of the Ministry of Defence slapping on a D notice, which would stop publication. Then, if they could break through the barrier and reach one of the Sunday newspapers with their version of the truth, they would have reached some form of sanctuary. "Reuters? United Press?"

"No," Middlemass said. "You plant the story in *one* newspaper. That's the best way to build up a story. One newspaper gets a scoop. So the others feel cheated and they work like hell on it."

"No bloody wonder you're a millionaire," Max said. Even in this situation, Middlemass knew how to play on the fears and greed of other men. "I know a character on the *Evening Standard*. One of my mates at art school. He's a layout man."

"A layout man?" Todd was fascinated. "You mean the newspapers got their own heavies?"

"He's called a subeditor or something," Max said.

"Fine," Middlemass said. "We want it in the last edition only, so that the dailies pick it up. I'll give you the line, then you and Shona can work on it." He was giving them the main points when Todd interrupted.

"That's it. Make it a great read for The Whore's Gazette. *Ban this filthy fucker now.* Red hot stuff, right? Coz we'll all be wearing wooden overcoats when it gets printed."

Middlemass had been expecting trouble from Todd, he was even hoping for trouble from Todd. From here on in, this compulsive killer was more dangerous than useful. Middlemass could never cheat this man or ditch him. Nor could he stop Todd from cheating himself. "You've got a better plan?" he asked.

"Too true, nob. Piss off outta here and keep on moving."

"Any particular direction?"

"London," Todd said. "We can make it in an hour or two and then get lost."

Middlemass was relieved for himself and sorry for Todd. "That's what they'll expect," he said. "So I'm heading southwest for the moment."

"Not me, nob."

"And what would you do with the prisoners, Todd?"

"Same as they'da done to us."

"Sorry," Middlemass said. "I need them as hostages and I think Radford will tell me more things I need to know."

"I got you," Todd said. "You're bloody Batman, aren't you? And I'm just a bloody sergeant footslogger. Can't even walk on the water. Can I have the folding money now?"

"You'll take a chance with the Daimler?"

"Gimme the money and I'd risk a byke."

"Fine. But there's one last job," Middlemass said. While he explained, Shona and Max were hovering. "Go and work on that newspaper story," he said. "Go and comfort the dog."

Once they'd gone, Middlemass and Todd dragged the Sky Eater from the ambulance. As he slumped on the floor of the barn, Todd delicately broke his fall then dragged him to the Daimler roughly, a sack of potatoes.

Middlemass made sure that Radford saw him hand Todd the .358 revolver. "Not here, somewhere outside. And muffle it if you can." Middlemass pitched his voice so that Radford ɪould hear.

Todd drove the Daimler outside. He got out, warned Max and Shona, left Wainright in the car and fired the .358 into a bale of straw so that the sound would carry to Radford and not far beyond. The Sky Eater still looked bad so Todd checked on his breathing and his pulse rate in case he'd died of fright.

Middlemass was in the rear of the ambulance, sitting in the nurse's chair when Todd came back.

"You reckon I couldda been heard?" Todd asked.

"Don't think so. Very quiet. A good clean job."

"Dead messy if you ask me," Todd said. Never knew Wainright *had* all them brains. Grey matter going spare all over the place. Some clean-up job for some poor bastard. Wouldn't fancy it myself." Todd sounded distressed. "Hard place to get at," he said. "Even the rats won't get no chance to lick it up. You want me to move?"

"Soon as you like," Middlemass said. "Radford looks a little waxy, doesn't he?"

"Bound to, inhe? Straight from the Chamber of Horrors, Madam Tussaud don't want him no more. Might as well melt him down. Best of luck, nob."

"Same to you," Middlemass said. As Todd left, Middlemass cut the gag from Radford's mouth. "Never pretend to be dead, or unconscious, *Colonel* Radford," he said. "That's the defence mechanism of the less intelligent animals. And they rarely live to find it doesn't work. Let's talk a little more."

Todd tapped on the outhouse door with unusual delicacy, before he entered. Inside Max and Shona sat on either side of the dejected Barney. "I'm off," he said. "Meet you at the Dogs Home, maybe."

"You're crazy," Max said. "You ought to stick with us." He was equally awkward.

"Not fucking likely," Todd said. "Hey listen. One thing I gotta ask you."

"Go ahead," Max said.

"I got to hide Wainright. And keep him alive, like."

"You'll manage," Max said, "he's not delicate."

"Yeah, that's not what worries me," Todd said. "But I gotta get my bent passport from the Elephant and Castle. Seems the mob down there have cornered the market."

"So?" Max asked.

"I gotta get it from Coalshop Charlie, the receiver."

"Don't look at me," Shona said, "I don't know all my father's friends."

"But he's a gangster," Todd said. "On the retail side."

"And what do you reckon we are?"

"You don't get it, do you? Gangsters are patriotic, dinnen you know that?"

"No," Max said. "I had a protected childhood."

"Dead keen on the Queen," Todd said. "Two things they can't take are pimps and . . . well, traitors, like."

"Don't tell them what you are. It doesn't show. Best of luck, Sweeney."

"Same to you." Todd was embarrassed, he moved from foot to foot. "Take care of him, will you, Miss?"

Max followed him out. "Don't go," he said. "You won't make it on your own."

"I've eaten camel shit and drunk sand in my tea," Todd said. "You better worry about yourself."

Barney slipped his collar and bolted. As Todd took aim with the .358, Max knocked his hand up. Todd's reflex was so fast and he didn't fire and the dog vanished into the bushes.

"You'd have made too much noise," Max said.

"You reckon? Saving that dog maybe cost you your life."

"I don't buy that," Max said. "Barney'll go back to Rookwood. Dogs don't talk, not even that one."

"Maybe he coulda learned from somebody like you. Don't know how you're gonta live without that hound." Todd was smiling, though, really smiling, that old undipped beam that Max had not seen in a long time. "Middlemass, he's all for it, inhe? Don't stick too near him, you might get drowned in his blood. Keep clear of him and live long enough to get stitched to his daughter. She's all right . . . for an American."

"What you talking about, Sweeney?"

"You know fucking well," Todd said. "You and me. We've been in it together for so long that we coulda gone on the halls as a mind-reading act." He held out his hand and Max took it. Todd's smile was widening and Max was looking at those ragged teeth for the last time.

28

"You're driving," Middlemass said. "I'm staying in the back with Radford."

"Great," Max said. "That's one problem solved."

"My driving's not that bad." Middlemass touched the delicate tip of his nose, showing the ring on his finger. "That's my lucky charm."

"Ever heard of Mike Hawthorn?"

"The racing driver? He was dead when you were five or six years old."

"Exactly," Max said, "but I've read about him. He always wore a black helmet and a light green jacket. He always pulled his socks up and turned them over twice before he started racing in one of those traffic jams at 120 miles an hour. He always climbed into a car from the right hand side. Then one day he ran out of road . . . a road like the Tolchester Road and not too far from here."

He knew that his anger was exploding in the wrong direction. He was equally aware that Middlemass was thinking of something else.

"What road would Todd take to London?"

"You know what road. I'll bet you asked him. The A.30. He'll keep away from the motorway."

"Yes," Middlemass said, "so we take the A.30 too. Toward London for about twenty miles before we head southwest."

"What?" Max's emotions were so mixed that he couldn't disentangle them. He was aware of anger, incredulity and something close to hatred.

"Cool it," Middlemass said. "If Todd gets through, we all get through. If they stop him, they won't expect us."

"You know something?" Max asked. "You remind me of that Hungarian who could get in a revolving door behind you and get out in front."

"I'm from Moravia. Don't insult me."

"I wish I *could* insult you," Max said. "You like to follow the people who follow you. Now we get a slight variation— you're following Todd. I could have worked that out if I'd been calm enough. And if I can, mate, so can Brigadier Murray-Strachan. Don't think you'll take him the way you took his local yobs. You won't."

Middlemass had expected Max to crack, but not this quickly. A word of encouragement might help. "You're learning," he said, "but Murray-Strachan won't be on the spot. Not yet."

They were ten miles up the road when police cars went raging past with their disaster bells tolling and their accident signs flashing. Fortunately there wasn't an ambulance among them or the scrapyard ambulance would have been recognised and they'd have been trapped. *Another thing Middlemass didn't work out,* Max thought, *he's getting reckless.*

Fifteen miles up the road, Max saw the red triangles and the winking signs to indicate a road disaster. "Get down," Max said, "right down." But Shona ignored him as he turned on his siren, set his blue lamp rotating and put his foot down on the boards. Then the police foot patrol waved him through.

The Daimler was burned out, almost on the crown of the road and there was no sign of wounded men being treated. Max swerved past the wreck and kept thundering on. He hoped that the police would think he was carrying an emergency case. Certainly they did not try to stop him or send a motorcyclist after him.

"You figure Todd could survive that?" Shona asked.

"No. But if he did, the Frighteners got him."

"How did they make it such a mess? Windshield shattered and the tyres flat?"

"Scatter-gun stuff through the windscreen and the tyres," Max said. "Very crude, very unsubtle. But it works." He was so angry that the ambulance almost took off. When he braked to make his right-hand turn to head southwest, the ambulance reared.

"Steady," she said. "Todd took his chance."

"He'd no chance in Radford's car."

"He figured he had and you're not his officer anymore."

"Too right," Max said, "he's remustered under the fellow in the fork and tail. I hope to Christ that Wainright's down there with him."

"And you'd like my father there to keep them company?"

"You asking me or telling me, Shona?"

"Stop it. Will you? Please? You're driving like a nut and you have to get by with my father. Not for long maybe. Maybe a day or two. Slow down, will you *please* slow down? This is a used car, Max. You want a blowout, too? You figure the brakes are up to this?"

Max took his boot off and the engine stopped screaming for oil. "You've got to make a deal with Dad," she said. "You've got to."

"That's right," he said. "I've got to ask him for your hand in marriage, haven't I?"

"Not before you ask me first," she said. "Why are you laughing? Hysteria or something?"

"No," he said. "Wonderful, isn't it? A shotgun courtship and your father came, too."

"Don't talk that way," she said. "You think about Todd all you want. Talk or stay silent if you want to. But . . ."

"But what?"

"Don't get it mixed up with us."

Middlemass was banging on the metal so Max turned off the road and battered up a forest track before he stopped. He was running over hidden treestumps and he had a fair chance of damaging the track rods and the steering but he didn't care. His old instinct for cautious driving had deserted him, he had a feeling that he was running out of road, wherever or however he travelled now.

As Middlemass came round the side, Shona got out and walked away. "I'm sorry," Middlemass said to Max.

"Ballox. Sweeney's dead and his blood's worth an hour to you. Sorry be fucked."

"I said I was sorry," Middlemass said, "and I'm sorry I can't oblige you with a fight. Some other time. Right now I want you to walk back to the telephone box and call the newspapers. Take Shona." As he went over the story they had to tell, he ignored their ideas.

"All right, sir," Max said. "You're the tycoon. We're the press agents. Anything else, sir?"

"Make that call collect."

"Reverse the charges? You down to your last oil field or something?" Shona stepped between them.

"It's all right, Shona. Just call collect, as I said. Or the newspaper won't take you seriously."

"And what will you be doing, boss?"

"Working out where we go from here."

"Won't you be praying through the night with Chaplain Radford?"

Again Shona got between them. "Radford? He fell out miles back. Didn't you hear the bump?"

Max understood but he refused to show it. "Thought you wanted more information?"

"I've got enough."

"Thought you wanted hostages?"

"Not any longer. Not after I saw the Daimler. Make that call collect."

29

BEFORE THEY SETTLED for the night, they swept the approach with fire brushes, wiping out their tracks in the shingle path to the church.

"How the hell did you know about this place?" Max asked.

"I study the maps, I read the guidebooks," Middlemass said, "I'm one of those eager American tourists." The flint church on the hill was the least-tended building in the hamlet. Down below, tiles were slowly sliding down the roofs of cottages that the owner wasn't allowed to demolish and didn't want to sell. So he was leaving wind and rain, rot and ivy to settle the issue out of court and he wouldn't have more than a quarter of a century to wait. "The English art of compromise," Middlemass said, "one of the qualities that made this nation great."

"Let's follow his example." Max dropped his fire brush.

"Keep going," Middlemass said. "Detection by footprint goes all the way back to Bible. Didn't you know that?"

"It's a closed book to me."

"I was raised on it, I was dyed in that vat. The Moravian Brethren grabbed me from the cradle."

"You made a remarkable escape," Max said. "And I still think we ought to keep moving."

"That's what they'll expect. Shona's tired. We're all tired. You want to walk all night?" The ambulance had been long abandoned, driven into bramble in a disused quarry, to rust with all the other rubbish in that unofficial tip.

"I still don't fancy sleeping in that church," Max said.

"Aggressive atheists never do."

"Why did you let Radford go?" Max asked. "Supposing he's fit to talk?"

"He won't be." But Middlemass looked embarrassed. "I could have killed him, of course. Could you see Shona helping at the secret burial?"

"No. But you needed him alive. You didn't get all the questions answered."

"Maybe I could have tortured him, so that it didn't show."

"I'll bet you're good at that."

"Competent, no more," Middlemass said, "but it's difficult to torture a man after you've been in a concentration camp."

"Now I'm with you." Max said.

"Are you? Can you imagine what it's like? Not only the torturers but the tortured get corrupted. I don't think I could torture a bug now." He couldn't remember the names or even the faces of the heroes of that camp. Who was it who'd written that the limepits of the world were full of unaccepted martyrs?

In the church tower, Shona was watching the glow in the sky. Somewhere close a farmer was burning his stubble. Then she heard the shotguns as the men beyond the fire dazzled the escaping rabbits in their headlights and shot them as easily as other men shot dice. Shona shivered although the night was mild.

"That you?" she asked as the church door opened.

"Come down and find a corner. Get some sleep," her father said. "Take over the tower, will you, Max?"

When the moon broke through, Max could see the pine-wood down below and it made him think of home. He'd never shared the southern English dislike for the softwood plantations they called coniferous slums, he was always happier on peaty soil, always preferred heather and ferns to grasslands. An old daydream came back as it had so often in Arabia. He was walking toward a rotting boathouse in the rain, smelling the acid niff of peat. In the ferns wrens were foraging like winged mice and a blue tit was hanging upside down, nibbling the blossom on a slender shoot. As the girl in the dream pulled a branch of silver birch aside, the backlash soaked him. In the dream the birch had been sharp enough but the face of the girl had been hazy. Now her face was clear, it was Shona's.

"Hear that bark?" Middlemass asked as he came up to the tower to relieve him.

"Vixen," Max said.

"Not the sound American foxes make."

"Maybe they're better mannered over there," Max said, "or maybe they're scared to bark."

"And maybe it's time for you and me to make a truce," Middlemass said.

"I was thinking that, too," Max said. "If we get out of this, well, Shona and me . . . you see what I mean?"

"I saw it some time ago."

"And you don't like it?"

"Would it matter if I did?" Middlemass asked. "She makes her own decisions. But thanks for asking. Anything about your family I ought to know?"

"Don't think so," Max said. "I'm the skeleton in their cupboard."

"Good," Middlemass said. "Anything you want to ask me?"

"Not really, but . . . nothing."

233

"But what?"

"I don't like people with money. Maybe you can't help having it, but money scares me. I need just enough to work out whether I'm going to spend it on booze or food. I like making momentous decisions."

"I'm sorry you're scared of money. A coward dies many deaths."

"Thought we'd signed a truce?"

"We're at the peace talks," Middlemass said. "You don't want to be scared of money. And you don't want to be so proud of being incorruptible. Money isn't the only thing that corrupts."

"I don't want power, either," Max said. "Except to do what I like."

"And isn't that the purest power lust?" Middlemass asked.

"I've met a lot of rich people, you know? They've spent so long making their pile, they've forgotten how to do what they like."

"Meaning me?"

"I don't know. Not now, maybe. You're getting a bang out of taking risks for high stakes."

Middlemass looked all around and listened carefully. Again the moon was obscured by cloud. "You should have kept that dog."

"It slipped its collar," Max said.

"After you loosened the collar. You think I'm in this for a gamble, nothing more?" Max handed over the Sterling Paget. "And if I win, I'll have a lot more money and that's all?"

"You tell me," Max said.

Middlemass checked the submachine gun.. "I'll try. Nobody ever figured I had a simple motive before. You're paying me a compliment, you know that?"

"Sorry. I didn't mean it."

"That's why I'm pleased. Now how about sleep?"

"Later. I was thinking about that newspaper story we phoned over. When they asked the awkward questions, I had to clear the line."

"You told them enough. They'll check with the local police." According to his drinking companions in the Rookwood Arms, the local chief constable lacked sophistication. As a young constable, he'd slapped his backside while he was riding his cycle and had fired imaginary six-guns in the air. He wouldn't stand up to the reporters' questions. "And you put them in touch with Laurence Adam." Middlemass would have liked to have seen them grilling the squire of Rookwood.

"Fine," Max said, "but that extra little commercial. The stuff we put over the phone. Both the British and the American governments being after you?"

"I'll tell you all about that in the morning. Sleep." Max stayed where he was. "What's the problem?"

"The Sultan of Doha," Max said. "When he gets the news, he won't sell to the Americans *or* the British. And you're supposed to be dead. So where does he sell his oil? Direct to the Japanese?"

"I've made a direct sale very difficult, all along," Middlemass said. "Almost impossible. Let's hope he sits on his oil. Until I get there."

"And if he doesn't?"

"He'll sell to Libya." Middlemass sounded as if he were answering a difficult child. "Get some sleep while you can. We have to be out of here before it's light."

"Libya? So you've gone through all this for nothing?"

Middlemass showed the illuminated face of his watch. "You want a lecture? Now?" Could Max see that American oil policy in the Middle East was just as crazy and just as

235

dangerous as the old British aims on the Gulf? When the British were strong enough to have aims?

"That's not possible," Max said. "Our Foreign Office is always wrong. That's called British way and purpose."

"Maybe Washington's jealous." As Middlemass saw it, America was still trying to tie up Doha with their other "allied" states of Persia and Kuwait on the Gulf. "The oil panic's on. But they're still hoping to hold the Gulf with this military and economic alliance, still trying to keep royal Arab backsides on Royal Arab thrones."

"But that can't be done," Max said.

"Even you know it, but they don't." Middlemass was certain that the traditional rulers of Saudi Arabia, Kuwait and Doha would soon be overthrown to join their royal cousins from Egypt and Iraq, Syria and Yemen, Algeria and Libya in exile or in death.

"But the Sultan of Doha can keep his palace a little longer if he makes an oil deal with Libya," Max said. "So you're still out on your ear."

"Why didn't you get to sleep while you had the chance?" Middlemass asked. "The new rulers in Arabia won't settle down with Persia for long. Might as well ask them to kiss and make up with Israel."

"I know that," Max said. "It's the Arabian Gulf to them, not the Persian Gulf. But . . ."

"When they stop fighting the Israelis or fighting off the Americans and the Persians, the gulf Arabs are going to get suspicious of each other again. And they won't have Libya as their natural leader, any more than they'd bow down to Persia or Egypt."

"I've got it," Max said. "Everybody fights everybody. So what happens to the oil?"

"They won't have a *real* war," Middlemass said. "On the

gulf, they're spending maybe five billion dollars on defence. Some defence. But it'll work. Just the way it works with the superpowers. The old balance of terror."

"Which suits you?"

"Of course," Middlemass said. "My interests and the general good just happen to coincide. If the Sultan sells to Libya, he's betraying my trust. So I'll have to make a deal with his successors. It'll take more time, maybe. But the oil stays in the ground. And it'll be worth a whole lot more when it comes out."

"After your time," Max said.

"I don't think so," Middlemass said. "I've read my horoscope another way." The feeling that death was at hand had deserted him as mysteriously as it had come. "But I do have to think about my investors and the return on their money. I may have to hurry up the march of time and get the Doha revolution started early." He was checking the Sterling Paget clips, apparently unaware that Max was shocked. "Shame about this gun. We're going to have to dump it soon. I'd like to know a whole lot more about it."

"You've been backing the Sultan *and* his rebels?"

"Naturally," Middlemass said. "I never take chances with other people's money?"

30

THE GOING WAS HARD in the morning and Max was weighed
down by fatigue. Middlemass seemed to be making for a busy
railway station in a crowded market town but he didn't
bother to explain how they'd cross the rash of roads to reach
it, once they'd left the woods. Shona was hobbling, her foot-
wear had never been intended for such a march, but she
didn't complain and her restraint made Max's irritation
worse.

"Which way now?" he asked Middlemass at the junction of
the tracks. Middlemass led along the track to the southwest.
"Civilisation's closing in," Max said. "We're running out of
woods." As Middlemass tried to relieve him of the submachine gun, Max tightened his grip on the shoulder strap.
"You can't swing from tree to tree in towns. It's against the
byelaws."

Two miles up the track, Middlemass waited for them, then
pointed. Once again Max grudgingly conceded his gift for
maps and ground. The heath ahead was dominated by a fern-
covered hill. When they reached the ridge, they lay in cover,
guarding all the approaches.

"Relax," Middlemass said, "we'll rest for a while." Max
folded his duffle coat to make a pillow for Shona. He watched

Middlemass position himself on the rise commanding the heath, he saw Shona settle, then his eyes began to close. . . .

He sat up abruptly as Middlemass set up the stolen radio set and put on the earphones. "You're not transmitting to Switzerland again?" Max asked. "You want the Frighteners to pinpoint our position?"

"Is it all right with you if I change the frequency? And listen to the radio news?"

The alarm calls of small birds woke Max and the first thing he saw was the kestrel, pulled slowly into the sky on its invisible string before it began its steep dive on its prey. Shona was gone, the sun was in the west, the best of the day had passed, he sat up quickly.

"Easy," Middlemass was higher, hidden by the ferns. "We're going nowhere in a hurry." When Max reached him, he tapped the SAS radio. "Who said they don't have advertising on the BBC?"

"They've broadcast our story?"

"On the hour, every hour. But Murray-Strachan's running his own commercial now." Middlemass's imitation of a BBC announcer was a brave try. "The police are anxious to interview two men and a woman in connection with yesterday's unexplained crash on the A.30 road, involving a Daimler car."

"Us?"

"With Identikit pictures in the newspapers," Shona said. "Built up by bystanders who just happened to be around."

"I'll bet they've got total recall." The "identikit reconstructions" of his own face and Shona's would be accurate. Middlemass' would not, for Murray-Strachan was hardly likely to link the A.30 crash with the story of Middlemass's death. "We're dangerous, I suppose?" Max asked.

"Very. The public are warned not to approach us. They

should contact their nearest police station." Shona's attempt at BBC jargon was better.

"Murray-Strachan's brighter than I figured," Middlemass

"And in a hurry," Max said. The brigadier was gambling on the police picking them up and keeping them under lock and key until one of his friends collected them. He'd certainly pinned them down. There was no chance now to pass unnoticed in a busy market town or a crowded train.

"Well, we can't live up here forever."

Middlemass spread his map. "See where we are? Not too far from Milton St. Mary's. Otter hunt there today. Laurence Adam told me all about it."

Shona's face showed as little enthusiasm as Max felt so he picked up a dead branch. "Otter hunters carry staves this length," he said. "They make a notch on them for every kill. Diaries, that's what they call their staves. You want to be an entry?"

"The otter hunt's the last place they'd expect us," Middlemass said.

"That was Todd's idea when he came to Rookwood."

"Look, Dad. Just because you've got a death wish . . ."

"I haven't. And a death wish is something you wish on other people. Didn't you read Freud in German?"

"I'll bet Murray-Strachan did," Max said. "The otter hunters, they'll be mob-handed. Bound to be. The same with the antihunting lot. Unlimited opportunities for accidents. And a whole battalion of policemen."

Middlemass marked up his map. "The police will be there. Not here. The meet's almost over, it has to be. So the demonstrators will be headed home. Students by the truckload." He drew a cross on the map. "That has to be the busy road." Max notched the dead branch with his fingernail. "You've got a better idea?" Middlemass asked.

"So we hitch a ride." Shona was trying to keep the peace. "And what's our story?"

"The students have been busy all day. They won't be reading newspapers and listening to the radio. What do they call themselves?"

"Hunt saboteurs," Max said. "That's the army I should have joined." Some of the anti-blood-sports student groups had tired of huntsmen beating them about, so they'd decided to retaliate. They'd begun with smoke bombs and firecrackers. Then, as the first generation of young Britishers who hadn't been called on to build a lasting peace upon the bayonet, they'd started swinging golf clubs, in the wrong game.

"Where could Shona be from? Someplace not too near."

"Warwick University? English department? They're strong on women's lib up there."

"And you?"

"I could pretend to be an art student," Max said. "How about you?"

"Do senior lecturers ever get involved?"

"Any kind of intrigue, they're involved. You'd better be a philosopher." Max was resigned and Middlemass made his last mark on the map before question time could begin again.

"We don't want to get there too early," he said. "I'm going to the road at that point and I'm going slowly." He picked up the SAS set, "Don't know whether I can tune in on the police patrol-car radios, but I can try." He handed Max the map and tapped his .358 revolver. "Give me half an hour before you start. If I hit any trouble, you'll hear it." He handed over the Sterling Paget. "Keep that for company but lose it when you see the road." He set off and didn't look back, then Shona began to make a grass skirt with ferns.

"Childish, isn't it?" she asked. "But I haven't had the chance since I was six."

"Wear it and you'll stop the traffic," Max touched her hair.

"Don't do that." She dropped the fern skirt, then picked it up and shredded it. "What was that song the children were singing?" she asked. "By the caravans? Ipper dipper dation, my operation . . ."
said.

"I can't remember," Max said.

"There's another one. Mickey Mouse is dead. He died last night in bed . . ."

"Forget it, just forget it. Try to blot it out." Max held her.

"Don't worry, I'm not going to crack up," she said. "What I'm trying not to say is . . . No, it's ridiculous."

"Say it."

"You know how a fly seems to know it's being watched? That you're going to squash it? I've had that feeling for hours. We're being watched. Somebody's waiting."

"Where and how?" Max asked.

"I told you it was ridiculous. You see more than I do in the country."

Max tried filibustering to rid her of this fear. "I used to walk about seeing nothing. Then there was this character. Fellow I met in a pub. A poet."

"A what?"

"It didn't show. Only line I ever heard from him was "I will arise and go now and get a Guinness free." But he knew the country. Always showing me things. Striped orchids. Sundew. He educated my eyes and ears, maybe. Mostly my eyes."

"So why are you staring at me?"

"The time of year, could be. Not too many orchids around." As she sat down he joined her, bodies almost touching. "I don't want to make love," she said.

"Me neither."

"I don't like things laid on for me."

"Exactly."

"That half an hour line of Dad's."

"Too obvious."

"Glad you agree," she said.

"So why are you blushing?"

"Maybe I've got things to blush about," she said.

"Me, too. Don't worry."

"I'd like not to, but some things I have to tell you."

"You don't."

"This British fellow in New York."

"Never heard of him."

"He was married."

"Lots of people are," Max said.

"Will you let me talk?"

"No," Max said. She heard the harsh cries from the copse beyond. "Some bird in trouble?"

"No, just jackdaws making trouble," he said.

"I've got to tell you this, I have to."

"Later," he said. Before he even kissed her, he was tingling. He stroked her hair and kept on stroking it. "This is fantastic, isn't it?"

"Yes," she said. "What I mean is no. We can't."

As he helped her with her clothes, he was astonished by what he found. Her shape changed with her clothes. Without them, she was even more beautifully proportioned. The legs became voluptuous above the knees. He was kissing them when he decided to kiss her all over.

"I thought the ground would be wet round here," she said.

"Should be. But it isn't. Very dry autumn."

"No, it isn't wet and I'm floating."

"You, too?"

"This isn't what it's all about, is it?" Shona asked. "For you, I mean?"

"I don't know what to say."

"The truth," she said.

"I've always told the truth to you," Max said, "it's a bit of a record for me."

"Try to break your record, then. Is this what it's all about for you?"

"No. I didn't think about it before it happened. My thoughts have been so bloody pure that . . ." He stopped talking.

31

THE FIRST TRUCKS went roaring by with police-car escort. Time passed and they grew anxious until they saw the small Citroën pickup with the sign KILL THE PIGS AND LET THE OTTERS LIVE. It was moving slowly and Shona flagged it down. The driver seemed to be travelling alone. He wore a camouflaged jungle hat, a dated piece of gear, in Max's view. "Who're you supposed to be?" he asked.

"We're with the heavy mob from Warwick," Max said.

"So how come you're this far down the road? They skipped out early." The truck behind them braked, it was loaded with students, the Citroën driver waved them through.

"We got lost," Max said.

"Everybody got lost. An absolute bloody shambles. Who's the old guy?"

"If you don't want to take us, shift," Max said. "He's a lecturer. What's it to you?"

"I'm a marshal."

"So where's your horse?" Max asked. "Piss off, brother, Pass on."

"I got to check, haven't I? You could be bogeys, for all I know." The driver saw that Shona was puzzled. "Policemen,

I mean. Doesn't she speak English? Get in the back. And leave room. My mates are further up the road."

Max pulled open the back. "What's this lot?" he asked.

"Thunder flashes, never got a chance to throw them." Nobody but Middlemass was aware of Shona's alarm.

"Firecrackers, that's all." He nodded to Max to get up front with the driver. The Citroën was really small, built for economy and known to Middlemass as a flying trash can.

"You'll have to shift back later," the driver said.

"I'll move," Max said. "What's your racket?"

"Obvious, isn't it, cock?"

"The daily grind, I mean," Max said. "When you're not working over otter hounders and Sir Jasper Jockstrap?"

"Fine art. So bloody fine you can't see it. Ilford," the driver said.

"That so? I was there for a while," Max was lying. "Who's the chief warlock nowadays? The illiterate turd who gives the longest lectures?"

"One-Ball Hall? He's still there and getting worse." Max settled back until the driver shook his empty cigarette packet. "Got a fag? No? Never mind. This is where I pick my mob up." The driver braked, dropped his empty packet and slid out.

"Me, too," Max said, "I want a piss." He wanted to check on the driver's friends and Middlemass had the same thought. As he followed the driver to the side ditch, the detonator functioned in the "empty" cigarette packet and the explosive charge erupted. The truck blew up and the flying trash can earned its name.

32

Max had been dropped from his battalion rugby side for trampling on too many senior officers. He was a fast spoiler, a natural marauder. But he couldn't gain on the Citroën driver although he was running on the pure gas of insanity. . . .

Then the man tripped. As he got up, Max got him in the neck with a rock.

After that he had no idea who he was or where he was or what he was doing, he was kicking the driver silly, using every dirty dodge the Parachute Regiment and Todd had taught him, until Middlemass dragged him off.

"No time to do it your way." Middlemass bent over the man, carefully moved a lock of hair, placed the muzzle of the .358 into his ear and blew his head off.

"How did he swing it?" Max was talking to himself. "He's a Frightener and . . ."

"He *was* a Frightener," Middlemass said. "Get down."

He ducked as the firing started. The round overhead was close enough to zip. That one was meant for Lawson and it found him.

33

EARLY ON MONDAY MORNING, Brigadier Richard Murray-Strachan was engrossed in Runciman's account of the Third Crusade. It was splendid stuff, of course, but it had been bad form of King Richard to refuse to pay homage at the shrines of Jerusalem after he'd made peace with Saladin. Murray-Strachan read until he found Runciman's appreciation of Richard as a bad son, a bad husband and a bad king but a gallant and splendid soldier. Murray-Strachan agreed with that, closed the book and considered the day ahead.

The chances were that the mood of the generals at the War Box conference would be fairly grim but no one could blame Murray-Strachan for the shambles.

At the beginning, he'd even communicated some of his doubts to Sleet but he didn't think the American would feel grateful. It wasn't Sleet's fault that the running battle had moved so fast, he'd never had a chance to find out where it was. Come to that, he didn't know where Sleet was and that man would have to be watched. Even the reports were conflicting. According to one, Sleet had been recalled to Washington in disgrace. Another suggested that Sleet had gone to Doha. Neither seemed particularly probable. Sleet had ample evidence that his British buddies had not been outstandingly helpful and he would know better than to involve himself directly with the Sultan of Doha. That crafty old despot had probably intended to sell his oil to Libya all along, using the Middlemass operation as a blind. If so, the report of the American investment banker's death had given him the excuse he needed.

Libya *seemed* to have profited, time alone would tell. The one country that had lost was the United States. Arab oil would soon hurt their economy and policies and pride, before they even begged a quart or two from Doha. From this moment, perhaps, the decline and fall of the American empire could be dated.

In fact, Murray-Strachan's plans had gone a fair way toward realisation. He had done great mischief to the Anglo-American understanding as he had intended, for the brigadier had long been committed to the nobler concept of a United Europe. He had almost destroyed the standing of the Special Air Service, which had been his chief military objective. Murray-Strachan detested the SAS, he abhorred the idea of a funny-nosed praetorian guard, more like the SS than the SAS. They had been perfectly okay in wartime but after the war they should have been disbanded with the other fancy forces.

In fact, they might even carry a little of the onus for the cock-up over Doha, share it with the Foreign Office, so to speak. No senior general who had attended Brigadier Murray-Strachan's original briefing would be likely to have forgotten his reservations and his doubts. By now his men would have placed the news that Radford had been a civilian forced upon him, against his will.

Murray-Strachan resisted the temptation to think ill of the dead. Perhaps it was just as well for all concerned that Radford cracked his skull when he fell from that ambulance.

Murray-Strachan remembered that he'd lent Radford his copy of *Josephus on the Jewish Wars* but that would be easily replaced.

Wainright. The brigadier spared the Sky Eater a passing thought, he wondered how that Boyhood-of-Raleigh face would look in death, after he'd been accidentally ambushed by his own men. All the evidence suggested that he'd been with Sergeant Todd and it was odd that Todd's body had not yet been recovered. But there was no need to mention Todd at the conference, or Lawson, come to that.

Middlemass' capture was imminent, perhaps before the conference began. The stuffed sparrow hawk phase was over. The brigadier would require all his delicacy and tact if he were asked about the sparrow hawk. It would be most un-seemly if some senior general laughed.

The loss of the Doha oil to Britain was the tricky issue, the British oily boys had moved without the necessary guile and speed. Again that wasn't Murray-Strachan's direct concern. And Arab oil was no longer quite so vital to the British. With the North Sea supplies and oil rationing to chill extravagance, Britain would be as self-sufficient as any other power for as long as world oil resources lasted.

Adam. He'd almost forgotten his appointment with the luckless squire of Rookwood. He'd have to warn Adam on where he stood in terms of the Official Secrets Act and re-mind him to forget that Shona Middlemass had ever lived. If student demonstrators played with fireworks, what should they expect?

The brigadier broke two eggs into a pint mug, beat them briskly, added milk, beat the concoction into a froth, drank it, then carefully washed his face and hands again. He checked his watch against the electric clock, took his bowler and umbrella from the rack, then left the house, closing the door quietly lest his wife's sleep should be disturbed.

Then, at the appointed hour, the brigadier walked to the railway station with the tip of his umbrella beating out the time. Some senior soldiers in intelligence tried to look like civilians but Murray-Strachan suspected that they fooled no one but themselves. It was different for junior men but one couldn't wear a cloak and a funny nose in one's own village at one's age. So Murray-Strachan's city suit was immaculate, his bowler was brushed, his shoes caught the sun and his umbrella was furled like a flag.

At the station, senior commuters nodded to him respectfully and he acknowledged by tipping up the point of his umbrella as he would have acknowledged a military salute.

As the train pulled in he got into his normal corner seat of his normal compartment and cracked open his *Daily Telegraph*. He couldn't bear to read the front page. Despite the warnings and the D Notice, they were still on about the death of this American, the accident on the A.30 and the otter-hunt explosion. Some of the yellow tabloids had even tried to trace some connection between the events. The brigadier decided this was a time to read the diary, to do the crossword and ignore the rest. . . .

As the carriage door opened Murray-Strachan was aware only of a bowler hat not unlike his own. He quickly dropped his eyes. That damned fool Lacey, the new man in the village, skirmishing again. The brigadier looked at the *Telegraph* diary but he couldn't read, he was so annoyed that the print was dancing. Time passed before he realised that Lacey had not spoken.

Murray-Strachan lowered his newspaper slowly, took in the bowler, then the face. He was staring into the eyes of John Middlemass.